DANIEL:
The Boy the Government Wanted to Kill

by

William Arcadipane

DORRANCE
PUBLISHING CO
EST. 1920
PITTSBURGH, PENNSYLVANIA 15238

Dorrance Publishing Co
585 Alpha Drive
Pittsburgh, PA 15238
Visit our website at *www.dorrancebookstore.com*

ISBN: 978-1-6495-7076-5
eISBN: 978-1-6495-7016-1

I dedicate this story to my son Salvador Banguela Arcadipane.
It was his inspiration.

I want to thank my wife, Julia Banguela, for being.

Maxine Andrade for helping,

Pat Hannon for listening,

and Phyllis Cardona reading.

-1-

L ET ME BEGIN WITH THE PROBLEM. We were cornered in our town in California. The government had surrounded us, we were declared a terrorist cult to be arrested. Really, the government just wanted to kill us. Believe me they tried. They missed their chance, as our psychic powers grew, we became untouchable. How this all happened is a crazy story, a story of love and innocence the government couldn't understand.

My brother Daniel asked me to write what happened even though it makes the rest of humanity seem quite absurd. He feels it is important to leave a record of our incursion in human evolution. The human race should know we were here.

My name is Kathy, I'm Daniel's sister and I hope what I am writing will be of some value. I want to point out we have survived because of our mental powers derived from our understanding and connection to the universe. We just couldn't convince the government we meant no harm.

A NOTE TO THE READER:

I was eight years old when it all began. I was eighteen when we began downloading all the US Governments files plus all their emails. We reviewed the data to make sure we were safe. Sometimes our analysis wasn't timely and we missed opportunities to prevent attacks, but that is what happens when there are thousands of items to review daily. We also hoped to gain some understanding of why the government hated us. I have spliced into this story emails I believe will give the reader a good idea of what the government was thinking. The emails reveal motivation and stupidity, judge for yourself.

This story is not in chronological order.

⁓⁓⁓⁓

Many years ago, my family found an alien stranded on Earth and he chose to hide in our shed. Why our shed? Chance, or maybe luck? It was as if he knew we would help him. His name is EL. We fell in love with him. There is no way to describe him; he just was. It was as if we already knew him, and the love he had for us we had experienced before. It was absolutely amazing how my brother Daniel linked up with EL mentally. They shared each other's thoughts, communicating without words and were able to experience each other's feelings. Daniel and EL actually became one mentally and spiritually. The world Daniel understood became universal. You could see the change in him; he seemed to have downloaded EL's being.

EL was amazed at how Daniel's mind opened and absorbed the relationship. He had never encountered this in any human being in all the centuries he had visited Earth. EL could see Daniel represented a new form in the evolutionary cycle of man. It is as if Daniel is the human version of EL. Even after EL left he was still present in Daniel.

It was strange but nice having EL around. I often played with him in my room. I was only eight and a little silly. I dressed EL up like one of my dolls, and we had tea together. I really loved him. EL was from another planet, stranded on Earth and just wanting to go home. We didn't know it, but all the time EL was with us, the government was hunting him.

Email to Washington:

We have located the general area where the alien is hiding. We are using sound trucks to listen for conversations about it. I am convinced the alien has contacted friends who are protecting it. How else could you explain our inability to lo-

cate it? We know it is in this vicinity. There are probably sleeper cells of aliens all over the planet just waiting to take over.

Email from Washington:

Remember we want it alive. A team of doctors are en route to your locations. They will start examining it as soon as it is captured. You may be right; how else could it elude us all this time. We'll deal with that later, just capture it.

The government had hundreds of men with highly sophisticated electrical devices trying to locate EL. They rode up and down our streets listening to everyone's conversations. They had a good idea he was in our neighborhood, but didn't know exactly where.

EL was wonderful to be with; you can see a whole movie about us. (The movie by Stanley Stainer, is really very accurate and not exaggerated. You can see how we enjoyed our time with him.) EL told us where he came from and showed us amazing things like levitating objects and constructing electrical instruments. He could manipulate matter and make things fly. He was so warm and loving. Everything he did was meant to help us, even though he was the one who needed help.

Unfortunately, the earth's atmosphere was not the best for him; his health was deteriorating and we didn't know what to do. We helped him construct a transmitter from simple toys in order to send a message to his people. Secretly it was placed in a remote area of the forest, not far from our home, hoping it would not be discovered. EL was sure the signal would reach his people and they would rescue him. He knew he couldn't survive for long.

EL was becoming weaker. His breathing was labored, his skin was becoming pale, and he could barely speak. We didn't understand why he was getting so weak. We saw how much power he had and figured he could do anything. We were just kids and knew nothing about death. We couldn't understand why his people hadn't responded. We became aware the government had an army after this one lovable person. I was just eight and I knew it was wrong, they weren't looking for him to be his friend.

For several weeks we hid him in our home. Mostly he was in Daniel's room but he stayed with me also. We had to be very careful, the government was all over the place.

Email to Washington:
_____

We have located the alien. Do you believe there is a family hiding it? We have proof that they are caring for it. They are probably aliens also, but like you said, we will deal with that later. The house is completely surrounded and we are preparing to go in. The medical team is standing by with all the equipment. Do we need a warrant?

Email from Washington:
_____

No warrant needed! This is a matter of National Security. Just go in and get the alien and anyone else that is involved. We may have to do some explaining later, but it is always better to shoot first and explain later. Make sure that alien family is thoroughly investigated. Go easy with them until we have some proof that they, too, are aliens.

Unfortunately, the government narrowed their search down to our house. They burst in with guns, screaming and pushing all of us outside. They were wearing space suits with breathing tubes attached. It was an ugly scene, especially the way they grabbed EL. We were screaming they should "leave EL alone; he was sick and means no harm to anyone." But they didn't care; they took him, threw him on a table, hooked up electronic equipment, and started poking his body. The doctors said he was too weak to transport, so, they erected an operating room right next to our house. It was incredible how quickly they constructed tents all around our property with rooms and tons of equipment. There were at least fifty doctors wearing white coats sticking needles in EL. It was chaotic.

Email to Washington:

ALIEN CAPTURED! It is very weak. Have set up the equipment here. Will transport it to Washington when it is stronger. We have already hooked the alien and Daniel to monitors. Oh, I told you the family where aliens. There is one of the kids, a twelve-year-old, communicating with the alien mentally. His name is Daniel. We hope the alien lives, but if not we at least have this Daniel to play with. The doctors said they have never seen anything like the link between this kid and the alien. We are already taking samples of tissue and blood from both. We plan to take samples from Daniel's mother, sister, and brother, but not now. They are not going anywhere. I will forward you a complete report tomorrow.

EL was very weak, but the government still wanted to experiment with him. They were actually going to cut him open, but he died. Daniel felt his death and collapsed and began to cry. Daniel had also been hooked up monitors and a group of doctors were working on him. When EL died everyone could see the link between Daniel and EL was broken. The doctors said EL had been controlling Daniel's mind, so they unhooked him. Daniel got off the table and ran to my mother.

Email to Washington:

The alien son of a bitch died. We did get a lot of data from the electrical equipment. We have brain waves, x-rays, and we have blood samples. We also have the kid that was telepathically communicating with the thing. Will bring the alien's body to Washington. We are making plans to deal with the kid and his family. The doctors are saying the kid was not telepathically communicating with the alien. They are saying the alien was actually controlling the kid's mind. We will see. I'm sure that kid and his family are aliens. When we have all

the data analyzed, we will move to confront that family.
There is no way a family just takes in a creature that ugly
and cares for it. They must be aliens.

The government placed his body in a refrigerator, and started dismantling the camp. While EL was in the freezer, his people communicated they were coming, instantly he came back to life.

Daniel telepathically received the message and ran to help. In order to get EL away from the government Daniel went to our brother, Mitchell. Mitch called all his and Daniel's friends together. They had to get EL to the clearing in the forest to meet his ship. We were so happy, finally EL's family was coming.

Mitchell and Daniel gathered their friends and snatched EL from the government. After a crazy chase they got him to the forest on their bikes. The funniest part was when the boys flew with him on their bikes. My brothers, Daniel and Mitchell, with their friends Gary, Tom, Stan, and Vinny, I was too young. You should have seen it, as the government agents closed in on the guys, EL in a basket on Daniel's bike, they all flew right over the heads of the Federal agents. All of them just gliding in the sky. They said they kept peddling in the air, it probably looked dumb.

Email to Washington:

The alien escaped and made it to his ship. He was helped by a
bunch of teenagers led by that Daniel. He organized the kid-
napping and made their escape by flying over our blockade
on bicycles. Yes, they flew on bicycles. I was there and wit-
nessed the whole thing, otherwise I would never have believed
it. They brought the thing to his spaceship. Once there, there
were tearful goodbyes, all kinds of hugging and crying. One
of our agents was there and witnessed it. I will forward a com-
plete report this evening. You see, I am right, they are aliens.
How else could they have flown on bicycles? We better arrest
all those sons of bitches. They were here on Earth all the time.

A sleeper cell planted by the aliens. We have our work cut out for us. There are more aliens than just that one family, I'm sure. There were a whole lot of kids helping it escape. This whole town may be the center of the alien conspiracy.

I arrived by car to the forest with my mother and Kiel—an FBI agent who liked my mom—in time to see what looked like a large star come gently down near the transmitter. I knew where the boys were going, when EL came back to life, the boys told me they were going there, they said not to say anything. But I had to tell my mother so we could go say goodbye.

At the spaceship I hugged EL and so did my mother and my brother, Mitchell. We all cried, including Kiel. When EL said goodbye to Daniel, they hugged and EL put his hands on Daniel's temples and told Daniel, "I'm always with you." That is when Daniel changed. I don't mean the way he looked or anything. Not even the way he spoke, it was just that after EL held him, Daniel was different.

El and Daniel held on to each other for a long time. (EL actually invited Daniel to come with him) but at last EL turned and boarded the spaceship waving as the portal closed. We stood there crying and waving while quickly, in almost an instant, the ship rose and EL was gone. We all just stood there hugging and crying. When the government agents arrived, boy were they angry, but Kiel calmed them down. Kiel was a high federal officer who identified with us, (really he liked my mother). Daniel commented, "it was easy to love EL; he loved and respected all living beings."

Email from Washington:

What do you mean the alien got to its ship and took off with the help of the kids? Arrest those little sons of a bitches and their families. That is obstruction of justice, interfering with the performance of a federal officer. How dare they? Who do they think they are playing with? You may be right; they may all be aliens planted here waiting to take over the earth. How the hell could they even pull off getting the alien away from you? You have over two hundred men. Where the hell were they? Where the hell were you? I now have to explain to the President that a bunch of kids outmaneuvered the best agents from our organization. I hope I won't sound ridiculous when I tell him we believe that the Daniel kid and his family are aliens working with the space traveler. You just better find me proof. I don't care what you do, get me proof.

After EL took off, we were proud to have helped him, congratulating each other as we returned home to celebrate. The police clearly didn't understand. They just wanted to capture him and experiment. They had no respect for him as a living being. As we saw it, we were just protecting a wonderful, lovable, different kind of person.

Tom, Gary, Stan, Paige (Daniel's "girlfriend") and Vinny all came back to our house. We laughed at how dumb the police looked when the bikes rode right over their heads. I didn't fly, but the boys did and they all said it felt strange. I did see the police with their mouths open as the boys flew over.

Email to Washington:

We are preparing to arrest the families. Our entire force as well as the local police are in place surrounding their homes. We can see that the bastards are celebrating their victory. But not for long. We will isolate them and make them talk. Transport is in place and our special facility here in California is ready to receive them. We have the medical staff standing by. We can also do more DNA testing on the entire group.

Do we need a warrant?

Email from Washington:

I don't think you should need a warrant, but our fucking attorneys pointed out that these are American citizens. They are in their own home. And, however foolish it sounds, our probable cause is that they helped an alien escape from government custody. We are telling the judge they helped a fugitive escape. I am not mentioning the alien part. I did mention it at staff meetings and realized some of our own people were looking at me with incredulity on their faces. We are selling the escaped fugitive to the judge right now so hold off till I get back to you. Wait for my OK. This is a matter of national security. When you get your hands on them, lock them up. Arrest anyone connected to the escape even their families. We'll get to the bottom of this. I did not mention to the President that we think this Daniel and his family are aliens. I will when you get me proof. We have enough egg on our faces after the escape.

Back home we had a party, played music, and laughed. We told and retold the story of what we had done. The boys loved the part where they flew over the police on their bikes. My mother ordered pizza. She was happy we had helped EL escape. Originally, we hadn't told her about EL, afraid of her reaction. We thought she would call the cops. But she was wonderful and loved him like we did. We were having a great party laughing and celebrating. We were just finishing eating when the door bell rang and in walked an army of police with guns drawn and a warrant for our arrest.

The police were very rude, and scary. My mother protested, but they didn't care. They told her to cooperate or they would handcuff her. Mitchell and his friends got loud and argued with the police. The cops told them to "shut up;" they did.

The government was angry we helped EL escape. Their warrants allowed them to search our house. We were a bunch of little kids and they had all those men and guns. They were not polite, with all that force they still kept screaming at us. Someone should explain to the police that when there is no threat, it is not necessary to act like bullies. They certainly didn't need that much force to subdue us.

The cops had an army of men to arrest a woman with her three kids— eight, twelve, and seventeen years old. There must have been a hundred of them, and they had big guns, I mean automatic rifles and handguns. They were wearing bulletproof vests, some read FBI, others said POLICE. Like what did they think we were? Terrorists? The nice FBI agent, Kiel, was with them. He tried to get the cops to lighten up, told them to take it easy and pointed out we were kids. He spoke to us nicely, reassuring my mother there was nothing to worry about. We were being taken into custody to be "debriefed." That is what they said, but it certainly felt like more than that. It was scary. I was tweeting one of my classmates when the cops grabbed the phone out of my hand.

The police took all the other kids outside and placed them in cars and drove away. We thought they were safe; they weren't. Later we learned they were driven to their own homes where they were subjected to the same ridiculous treatment for no reason.

The police ordered us to pack our bags, take what we would need for at least the next three weeks. My mother was nervous and started giving orders while crying. I packed my doll and a few changes of clothing for her along with my own things. My mother kept yelling instructions "don't forget your toothbrushes and underwear." All the time packing we were accompanied by two police officers carrying big guns. They were scary and very vocal, kept telling us to shut up and move faster. (And Daniel doesn't understand my aggressive attitude?)

When we were packed, they led us out at gunpoint into a waiting bus. We were pushed on board. Our neighbors were staring at us. Some of the kids waved, but most were too frightened.

It was really a nice bus. There were couches, a TV, and a refrigerator with plenty of food. There was a toilet. At first, we were tense, but then we relaxed, watched TV, and ate a lot of the food. My mother never really relaxed. You could see she was scared and kept asking Kiel for an explanation. Eventually, we all fell asleep.

A number of hours later, the bus finally stopped. We got out and found ourselves in a large walled park in front of a big brick building. The grounds were completely enclosed by high walls, cameras everywhere, and guards with guns. There were trees and a lake. It seemed like a nice place for a vacation, except for the guns, the walls, and the cameras.

We were led in and given a hot meal with lots of dessert. My mother said she just couldn't eat; she was too upset, but she listened to Kiel, who sat down with us and ate. Within a short time, our friend Gary and his entire family arrived, then Tom's family, then Stan's, Vinny and his whole family, with Paige's family right behind them.

They had gone through the same experience, arriving home surrounded by police with open weapons. They were served papers and ordered to pack. The working parents were arrested at their place of business and brought home. When everyone was accounted for, they were placed in the same kind of bus and driven to our location. The adults were very annoyed. We kids just laughed and talked about how cool the bus was with all the food and the large TV. The adults sat down, enjoyed the great food, bitching about how they were treated. They felt we were "subjected, unnecessarily, to very harsh treatment." The parents said they felt humiliated in front of the coworker and neighbors. They wanted to call their lawyers but had no phones.

Some of the parents blamed their kids for getting involved with Daniel and Mitch to steal a "what?" They couldn't believe what we told them.

Email to Washington:

We have all the involved families in custody and secured in a safe facility we use for special needs. You know it "Hyde Park." We will get to the bottom of this. I have a special team in place and they will do the interrogations. They won't stop until we have the proof we need. We will get the truth out of them. Most of the families are probably not aliens; they may be acting under the influence of that Daniel. Remember, he has telepathic powers. He probably enters their minds and convinces them to help him. I will get the proof we need. My recommendation is that we accidentally kill this whole group now. That may seem a little drastic, but I have a gut feeling about this. They are only waiting for the right moment to take over the planet.

PS: Agent Kiel may be a problem. He seems to be involved with the families. Particularly with Daniel's mother. I will keep you posted. There is one loose end that we are pursuing, Daniel's father lives in New Mexico. We will have him in custody shortly.

The government had us locked up; we could not leave the grounds. They kept repeating we would be well cared for and only be held for a short time. The adults kept complaining, but we kids laughed and talked about EL. The hospital staff showed us our rooms and tried to be polite, but under the circumstances, everything they did was annoying. Each family was given a large area with as many bedrooms as needed. The rooms had big windows with plenty of light, a great view of the lake and the forest behind it. The rooms were fully furnished except no TV, no radio, no computers, no telephones. We did have a refrigerator and a microwave. Each section had two toilets and two showers. The beds were big and comfortable. They even provided housekeeping services.

We would be eating all meals together in the dining room. We were introduced to a group of tutors, one for each kid so our education would continue. Our parents were annoyed. They were told not to worry, "all would be taken care of including the bills and their paychecks." In addition, all the "guests" would be paid for their cooperation.

OH! They kept apologizing for the "inconvenience." We could order whatever we wanted. I asked for a bed for my doll and they got me one. I must say some of the adults laughed at me when I asked, but after I got the bed, everyone came up with things they needed. They took full advantage of the situation.

Email to Washington:

These sons of a bitches think they are on a vacation. One kid asked for a bed for her doll. Daniel's sister, a little bratty bitch. Do you believe? Then all the rest put in orders for clothes and games. They think this is a joke. We'll show them.

That kid Daniel is in a coma. The doctors have no explanation. He seemed fine when we brought him in. On the second morning his mother called the doctors to come to his room because he was not responsive. He has been placed in a separate section of the building and a team of doctors are monitoring him around the clock. He is connected to electrodes and other specialized equipment. We will have our proof soon even if he never awakes. We are doing DNA testing. We'll proof they are aliens. The adults are very uptight. You can see that only Daniel's family was actually aware they were hiding an alien. But that doesn't explain away the cooperation rendered by their children in the escape. Remember all those kids were flying on bicycles. We must not let any alien escape us this time.

-2-

THERE WERE TWO BIG HEATED POOLS, one indoors and one outside, we used them frequently. It was fun having our own pools. There was a gym, two tracks inside or out. There was both indoor and outdoor tennis courts. The adults were very annoyed. They kept trying to talk to whomever was "in charge" but were told "in due time." They kept blaming the "whole mess" on my family.

Two days after our arrival several "doctors" came into the dining room and announced our "debriefing" was to begin. Each person was introduced to their interrogator and one by one we were led away. Everyone went into separate rooms where two doctors asked questions about EL. We were told everything was being recorded. They explained the reason for the interrogation was we might provide some details about EL, information we were not aware we had. This would help the government understand where the extraterrestrials came from and who they were. A few doctors said there is a possibility that our planet was in danger. I thought that was funny. It seemed to me the people who thought that about EL had the real problem.

Email to Washington:

The kid that was communicating with the alien is still in a coma. It seems strange to me he is suddenly in a coma. The doctors are reporting a great deal of abnormal brain activity. They have no explanation. I ask them did they think he is human? They looked at me like I was crazy. They said he was, but I don't believe them. They said the coma may be a result of "emotional trauma." There is a possibility "the alien had controlled" the minds of these kids. They are testing every angle. I have tried to get them to see our point of view. They simply reject any idea that these kids are anything other than human beings. You and I both know they are aliens. What more proof do these idiots need? They harbored an alien, protected it. They telepathically communicated with it, they flew. I say again, give me permission to kill them all, now before the whole planet is lost. I will push these so-called doctors to understand the obvious. That is one of the problems with overeducated people: they think too much and can't see the obvious.

We fell into routines. After breakfast, the interrogators picked us up in the dining room. It was the same for everyone. We walked to our rooms. On the way there was small talk. How are you today? Isn't the weather nice or lousy depending on the conditions. Once there, I took my seat by the blank wall, my "doctors" sat behind a desk with a mirror behind them. There was a refrigerator with sodas, milk, and juice. A coffee machine was in one corner. Everyday there was fresh fruit on the table with new yellow pads and six pens. We would enter, grab something to drink, and in a few minutes the questions would start.

The "doctors" asked questions for hours:

"How did EL know to come to your home for help?"

"How did your family signal him?"

"What did you feed him?"

"Did he teach you anything?"

We were always asked the same silly questions. I felt strange because I could feel Daniel's presence, I sensed him helping me. We all gave the investigators the same answers, the truth, but they didn't believe us.

Email to Washington:

They are all telling the exact same story. They don't even vary by one word. Even the little kids use the same words, and we have not been able to break them. It is not possible that a group of normal human beings can even coordinate a lie like this. Even if they rehearsed, there would be some variation in the story. The doctors say it appears like mass hypnosis. (Do you believe this shit?) How is it possible the alien hypnotized them and that is why they are all telling the exact same story? The doctors have stated the kid Daniel was not really communicating with the alien telepathically, but rather the alien was controlling his mind. They have found nothing to suggest any of them are abnormal. I've brought in a few more experts who are aware of the urgency of this situation. They have worked with us before and will get to the "truth." It is a little frustrating to say the least. With all these "brilliant doctors" they find nothing, while the truth is staring them in the face. My full report will follow.

Daniel helped all of us. When questions were asked, we not only said the same thing, we said it in the same way with the same words. We could sense Daniel had reached in and given us strength. I found myself analyzing the interrogators (realize I was only eight years old) but that is what I did. We all did the same thing. The doctors were annoyed; they felt we were lying. They said there should have been a greater variety of descriptions of what happened. It was not possible all of us had the same story, we "must be lying."

Email to Washington:

They are all lying. They have memorized a script and are sticking to it. We will get the truth out of them. If I could just physically beat them a little, they will find their voices. I don't buy that mass hypnosis bullshit. There has to be some way to prove they are aliens. Can I have the green light to use a little physical force? Maybe some well-placed threats. See what you can do.

Email from Washington:

GO EASY, be very careful. The congressmen and senators from California are raising hell. Also the ACLU has filed a lawsuit claiming their civil liberties have been violated. I have been called to give a full report. There isn't much I can say without evidence. We only have a short time left before the liberals make so much noise that we must release them. I will appear next week before Congress. The President has already indicated he wants them released. I was able to get a few more weeks. Come up with something or let them go.

I should mention, after we arrived Daniel had collapsed. He was taken to a separate area in the hospital and we were told he was in a coma. The doctors had no explanation and were conducting tests, "he was in no danger." They did say they were registering enormous brain activity. We prayed for him. While we were praying, we experienced Daniel thanking us and joining in our thoughts. We never mentioned our connection to Daniel to the interrogators. None of us did. It was special to us and none of their business.

The doctors thought we were coached. They were annoyed with our parents and wanted to know who came up with the "ridiculous" story. They could not understand how everyone's story was exactly the same? Did we plot the coming of the spaceship? Were we involved with its arrival? How did we contact them? The questions just went on and on.

Our relief came at lunch, eating our meals together, seeing each other broke up the day, and the food was good. We kids would laugh at the dumb questions. But our parents didn't laugh.

Our parents could not believe the government was so stupid as to think we invited EL to Earth for a visit. Like we used our cell phone and called— "EL, you should come visit California. We have great vegetation and you can come and almost die." It was so stupid. How could the government think we invited him? How could they not see we were telling the truth? How could they not understand we had no reason to make any of the story up? The very fact that all the questions implied that we were part of an alien conspiracy to take over the earth was ridiculous.

Email to Washington:

They are sticking to their story and we have not been able to break it. Can I use stronger measures? We have seen this before. All we need is to break one of them and the rest will follow. I think Daniel's mother is a weak link. With your OK I can make her bleed out the truth. It won't take much. A little threat to have one of her kids killed. Actually, I would like to get rid of her daughter. She is a real pain in the ass. Questions all the time and aggressive as hell. Just won't shut up. Our special group of doctors have come up with nothing. They do believe they are hiding something. They are also convinced they are aliens posing as humans. Like in that movie where the alien takes over a human body. That is why the DNA testing came back normal. Just see if I can go a little harder on them.

Email from Washington:

No Rough Stuff. Hands off, we may have a lot of answering to do to Congress for just what we have done already. We certainly don't want it worse than it is. As it is, we are among a very few people who recognize these kids for what they are. We will have to bide our time until we have proof positive and can get the right people on our side. For now they have to be released. Rest assured we will keep them under surveillance. I have set up a special budget for your use. Get everything in place so we will not lose sight of them. I want to know everything they do. I mean everything, even monitor their toilets. There should be no room in their homes where they can plot.

The only decent person we spoke to was Kiel. He would stop by often eating lunch and/or dinner with us. He said he enjoyed our company, (especially my mother's). The day was broken up for the kids by three hours of tutoring. But even there, odd questions were thrown in by the teachers. Some of the questions were motivated by curiosity, but others we could tell were looking to trick us. The teachers really knew their subjects and we enjoyed the lessons. I could feel myself growing inside. I could feel a greater understanding of myself and began to read much better. I mean really read. The other kids said the same thing. Oddly, we all enjoyed math the most.

About a week after our arrival, my father with his current wife, Sally, and their daughter, Sharon, my half sister, arrived. They had been located in New Mexico and subjected to the same rude treatment. They new absolutely nothing about EL, but that didn't matter. Mitch and I were happy to see them. My mother was civil. Best of all, I got to be with my sister, who was my same age. That's why they divorced. My father and his wife were very annoyed at being arrested blaming my mother for "not controlling her kids." This was quickly forgotten as they fell into the normal bitching all the other parents did.

Email to Washington:

Picked up Daniel's father. He and his family were living in New Mexico; they are now being interrogated. If there is any genetic link to the alien, we have them all in custody. One thing that is very interesting, the two daughters are only a month apart. Could mean something about their breeding habits...? I really do think that it is a mistake to release them. Really just let me have them killed. We could have a fire and they "accidently perish." I know you understand this is our opportunity to stop these aliens before they get too strong. See what you can do. I actually feel like just doing it and suffer the consequences. We must protect America.

My mother confirmed Daniel appeared to be sleeping when she visited with the other parents. The doctors had no idea why he was in a coma, but felt it would be good if the parents read to him and spoke to each other in his room. Only "grown-ups" were allowed to visit, but we could feel him within our thoughts. We discussed it among ourselves. We were communicating with Daniel and he with us. He was constantly helping us to deal with our situation.

The hospital was a big place, lots of guards, and everywhere you looked there were cameras. Most of the staff were just working people doing their jobs. You could see they accepted we were telling the truth. We got to know some of them. But others were just not interesting at all. They were nasty and condescending, treating us like we were always lying. They never saw us as human beings, to them, we were aliens, and they were going to prove it. You could tell they operated with a predetermined theory and they were going to find the evidence.

Email from Washington:

How is it possible you have nothing? Do you realize the amount of money we have invested in proving these kids are aliens? And you have nothing? I'm on the hot seat here. I have been called before several committees. Find something. But do not hurt any of them. If we don't release them soon, the President himself might just show up to check on how they are being treated. FIND SOMETHING!

To break up the routine and get away from the adults, many days we kids would go exploring in the woods. We walked and joked around the whole time. One day we went through these trees; it took about an hour to arrive at an opening. We couldn't believe it. We thought we found a way out. In front of us was a large hill. It appeared there was no wall beyond it. But no, as we climbed up the hill there was the twenty-foot-high wall with cameras mounted on top.

One of the kids said, "What could they do to us if we cut a tree down and put it against the wall and used it as a ladder? Would they shoot us?"

Just as he finished the words *shoot us* a voice on a loud speaker answered, YES! And laughed. That really scared the hell out of us. They could see and hear everything we did. After that we spent plenty of time together, playing, talking, but we lost any hope of escaping.

Our parents were upset, the government had some silly idea we contacted EL and invited him to Earth. How they could believe such a thing our parents kept trying to figure out. A check of our family trees would reveal none of us were aliens. Some parents blamed Daniel for causing all the trouble. They suggested my mother should have called the police immediately. They often describe their session with the interrogators and compared notes. It seemed silly to us kids, a real waste of time, talking about the same thing all the time.

We didn't have the same doctors; they rotated. What strange people the doctors were. They varied from truly interesting scientists, to jerks who thought every answer was a lie, even when I told this one guy my name, he would ask, "Is that really your name?" They just kept repeating the same questions over and over again. Daniel later told us the experience matured us. Mature or not, it was a terrible experience. I often think about how I felt they were hurting me and my family.

They performed many tests, hooking electrodes to our heads, using scanning devices while asking questions. We were constantly wired to machines while they thought of new ways to trick us. I asked what they were looking for? One idiot said they were afraid we had been exposed to radiation. They found nothing. Oh! They filmed everything. I don't think they had cameras in the showers, but who knows?

Strange how they thought a variation in response was an indication of a lie. Like when they asked me my name for the one hundredth time, so I gave them a different name. The doctor and her assistant went "Ah-ha! We got you; so Kathy isn't your real name. Who told you to lie? Where are you really from? How are you related to the alien?" This went on day in and day out. After that I stopped joking around with them. We did get to rest on Sundays. Well... we thought it was Sundays. We actually lost track of time. We had no TV, radio, newspapers, or cell phones. One of the parents made a calendar and posted the day and date at breakfast.

They felt it gave us a reference to our lives. It did come in handy for celebrating events like birthdays, anniversaries, and holidays. My mother jokingly had a cake made to celebrate the day she divorced my father. We thought it was funny, but he didn't. His wife thought it was hysterical and helped my mother blow out the candles. Every one took part in celebrations. They even took to inventing events to celebrate.

In the fifth month Daniel woke up. My mother came to the dining room and announced Daniel was back. She had spent a few hours talking to him and he seemed fine. He was a little "serious," but understandable given what he'd been through.

Email to Washington:

The little alien Daniel is out of his coma. Now we'll get some answers. We'll see if he tells the same stupid story as the rest of them. There doesn't seem to be any side effects of his coma. He immediately started chatting to his mother. We have all the data, the DNA, the electromagnetic data. Now that he can talk, we'll see what he knows and if he tells the same story as the rest. It is so strange we have noticed the entire group of kids like each other. They never get into arguments. They actually go around as a group, the young kids, I mean very young kids play and hang out with kids twice their age, playing games together. They are always all together. That is not normal. Most kids of different ages can't stand each other. I have mentioned it to some of the doctors. Their response is that under the circumstances, they only have each other. One even said I was making a mountain out of a mole hill. The nerve of that liberal. I'll keep you posted.

We were so happy Daniel was okay. The doctors immediately started to interview him. A month later, he joined us, he suddenly appeared at dinner. I screamed and ran to him. Daniel hugged each of his parents, especially our mother. When it came time to hug Paige the two of them just kissed like lovers. Boy were we surprised, I mean they were only twelve years old! The parents stared, many of the kids laughed, I blurted out "how disgusting."

Daniel was happy to see us, especially our father and sister. His return was a great moment. Daniel then hugged each kid individually holding our head in his hands, with his palms on our temples, and we just stood there crying. We all cried. It was not till later we understood what Daniel had done.

We had a thousand questions. What did they do to him? What did it feel like being in a coma? Did he realize he was communicating with us? Daniel answered every question in a matter-of-fact way. We could see my mother was right, he was very serious.

Daniel was happy to be with us, especially with Paige. Her parents just accepted their relationship. Gary's father asked if Daniel got the impression the government thought we had invited EL to visit us. Daniel said, "The government not only thinks we invited him, they believe we are aliens sent by him to secure the earth for our alien race. The government believes we are preparing for an invasion. We are the front line in the alien attack." We all laughed.

Now we were all together, it was wonderful. We noticed we could share each other's thoughts and feelings. I didn't have to ask a question to get an answer, communicating without words. We felt close to each other and shared in a personal way our feelings and the process of learning.

Email to Washington:

Yes, sir, we will follow up soon. They are to be released as ordered. If it were up to me, I would shoot them all now while we have them. Believe me, even though we have turned up nothing, I know they are aliens. They could have easily faked the DNA tests. But orders are orders. We, of course will keep our eyes on them. I have doubled the number of agents on the

case and increased electronic incursion. They will be released
as soon as all is in place. We are placing eyes and ears in
every room in every one of their homes. We are rigging the
radios in their cars so we can listen in to everything they say.
Thanks for listening to me on this and not asking for a war-
rant. I'm sure we wouldn't have gotten it. We know this is a
matter of national security. We must do everything we can
to protect our country.

One day at breakfast, a man we had never seen before identified him-self as the director of the program, Dr. Stewart Herbert. He spoke about how grateful they were to have interviewed us and how important our co-operation had been; the program "yielded a great deal of data." He apolo-gized for the "inconvenience" and hoped we felt we were well treated. The most important thing he said was in a few days we "would be released."

The director went on and on about how much they had learned and hoped in the future we would look back at our stay with fond memories. No further tests were planned, and we should be gathering our belongings. We were told to take everything, including what they had provided. He then invited us to attend a party with the staff to celebrate the completion of the mission.

At the party were the doctors, tutors, and some of the guards. It was interesting, the same doctors we sensed cared for us were relaxed. The in-different and accusatory ones were visibly upset. It was a festive mood, and most were glad it was over, but we could see a small group clearly hated us. They must have been ordered to attend the party.

Email to Washington:

All our equipment is in place in their homes and in the town.
Some agents have moved into their neighborhood. We have
audio and video in every room in their homes including the
bathrooms. You are right we must make sure they have no
private area in which to plot. The families are being released,

but we have good support among some of the medical staff. They agree there is something we are not being told. They strongly believe that the kids, especially Daniel, is probably an alien. It is amazing to see how everyone, including the adults, look up to him. Why would adults look up to a twelve-year-old?

A week later our departure day arrived. We were instructed to take everything. We had more than twice as much as we brought. The next morning, the same buses that brought us were waiting to drive us home. We were so happy we broke out in a cheer, even the adults.

We traveled in two buses. The parents let all the kids ride on one bus. The whole trip we goofed, talking about the hospital.

Daniel asked jokingly, "What is the easiest way to get a person to give up their morality, education, and identity?" We all gave our guesses. Finally, he said, "Tell them what they are doing is a matter of national security." We understood.

I felt like a celebrity, as we arrived in our town, friends waved and ran after us. It was great seeing them. It was fairly obvious to our friends Daniel had changed. He was thoughtful and responded clearly to any question. He laughed and joined in with us, but we knew he was different, and we all looked up to him, even the adults.

My mother blamed the change in Daniel's behavior on the way the government treated him. I asked Daniel if he felt different? He said he felt more aware of himself, seeing things much clearer. Daniel was twelve years old and he became our leader. We understood, including the adults—Daniel was our future.

Email to Washington:

They are back in their town. We dropped them there this morning. They know they beat us. You should have seen the cheers they let out when they left. They were all smiling from ear to ear. We will keep watch for our chance to wipe them out. Thanks for the increased funds; a lot was spent on the surveillance equipment. I will soon bring more agents on board. I'll be in Washington next week so we can go over our next offensive. We could arrange for them to have fatal accidents one at a time. In that way we can accomplish our goal of eliminating them and would be held blameless. It's just an idea. In a short time, we will have our proof from the equipment we have in place. We'll catch them discussing their offensive. Then we can eliminate them.

We were driven to our homes. They were in good shape, apparently the government had them cared for. The plants were watered and trimmed and the grass was cut. All the bills were paid. Our parent's jobs were waiting as if they had never left. Our parents received eight months pay without deducting the amounts paid for the bills. In addition, each household received fifty thousand dollars in cash to cover "the inconvenience." Our parents were happy with that. The government didn't apologize; they said it was necessary for "national security." We laughed. My father decided not to return to New Mexico; he wished to stay. So, my mother gave him and Sally Mitch's room. Mitch moved in with Daniel, and Sharon moved in with me. I thought that was great. We had become great friends.

At home it was good to have a normal breakfast. Ma made our usual: frozen waffles, lots of syrup, melted butter, milk, and orange juice. You would think we would be spoiled by the great food we received in the hospital. No! Ma's was best. I guess it had nothing to do with the quality of the food and all to do with just being home.

While we were laughing, Mitchell said he thought the government wasn't going to leave us alone. "It was clear somebody thinks we are aliens." We laughed; Daniel was quiet, looked up and said, "It has only just begun."

Daniel felt we were now a permanent target of the government. They would go on observing us every minute of every day. Ma said if we went back to our normal lives, they would leave us alone. We laughed, after what we went through, what was normal? We were looking forward to returning to school. We hoped that would be normal. In the meantime, being home felt great.

Mitchell was supposed to go to Stanford and study physical education, now he decided to study math. In fact, all the kids got into math and science, even me. I was suddenly able to read well and enjoyed it. I was reading fast with great understanding. Daniel said because of our experience with EL, we now had a greater awareness of ourselves and reading is one of those tools that furthers awareness. Our neighbors looked at us as celebrities. The kids wanted to be with us. Some parents were not so forthcoming and stopped their kids from associating with us. They just "didn't want to get involved." They had witnessed our arrest and read all about how we were aliens. Apparently, there was open discussion of our alien status in the media, attributed to an "anonymous government source."

I was one of the youngest kids, but I, too, was into the books. I could read anything and I understood what I was reading. Reading was fun, an inner experience, I could feel myself learning. I could understand also what the others were reading. It was strange realizing I could share silent thoughts with other kids.

In September it was great to get back to school. We moved as a group, only separating when we had different classes. The teachers commented it was like we were in a parade. In one of my classes, I was asked what I did on the summer break? I told them about the hospital. When I finished the teacher said she found my speech and vocabulary was of an educated adult. She asked, to what did I attribute that? I said it probably had to do with the private teachers in the hospital. I was put in a more advanced class. In the new class, I was given exams in reading, math, and science. My grades were so high, I was placed in high school. It was strange to be in high school at nine years old.

We would meet as a group after school usually at the library. Our whole town had changed. The parents became friendlier. And the kids were nicer to each other and much smarter in school, well, not everyone, some families moved rather than be exposed to the "alien freaks."

Email to Washington:

It is unbelievable the way these kids parade around town like zombies holding hands. It is not just the kids we rounded up and questioned. All the kids in the town have joined together. The adults too. I believe that Daniel has taken control of their minds. He is building an army. They are always studying. Granted, they are very intelligent, studying is not the problem. I swear they sort of tune into each other when they are together. We have noticed that one kid will read a book and like magic all the kids are discussing the book. It's the same with almost every topic. They are probably absorbing all our culture to make it easier to take over. We have a good number of eyes on the ground. Will keep you posted. The surveillance equipment we installed has shorted out. None of it is working. Those aliens did something. When we have a chance, we'll fix it.

After a year or so, the government agents stopped coming around. They seemed to have left us alone. All except Kiel, he was dating my mother. My father sold his house in New Mexico and bought one right next door. We were happy, Daniel, my big brother Mitchell, Sharon, me, Stan, Tom, Gary, Paige, and Vinny, who I wound up marrying when I got older. I'll tell you that later. We realized some of the teachers were not prepared to educate our group, but we respected them for their efforts. In fact, some of us started teaching the lower grades. The teachers enjoyed the experience and grew in their abilities.

Mitchell went to Stanford majoring in math, a few guys went with him. We were celebrities, everyone wanted to be our friends. They had questions, which we didn't mind answering. They wanted to know about EL and where he came from? What did he tell us? They were interested in our hospital stay. We freely told our story over and over again.

Our group became bigger. It came to include our entire town. About 30 percent of the town moved out eventually. Later, after college, we accepted many families that shared our values. Some wrote us and we would interview them. Some we met in our travels or in our businesses. Our town schools produced many great scholars that stayed on with us.

The whole town became a collection of interesting, intelligent people, a nice place to live, a big family. Even my father just fit in. It was nice to have my dad and sister around. Sally and my mother became good friends, doing almost everything together. Learning was fun; amazingly, I could feel my mind growing with understanding of who I was.

Daniel was amazing, he absorbed everything. He read every book. He even downloaded every research paper he could find on whatever topic. He not only reads them, he understood them and would explain them to us. We would get excited and before we realized it, we absorbed and understood what he read. Sometimes it was obvious one of us understood a subject in a wonderful way, with a passion, that person became the maven of the subject in our group. We would refer all questions to our maven.

Daniel said, "One of the problems in society is there is no way to recognize competence." People who really know can't compete with those who have "honest opinions." In our case we are constantly aware of what we know and what we don't know. We have opinions, but they are based on facts. Most people don't want to deal with facts and evidence. There seems to be a general belief that opinions, particularly "honest opinions" are much more important than evidence and facts. Even scientific facts are rejected if there is an "honest opinion," without factual basis, presented contradicting it.

The rejection by parents of vaccines for their kids is a good example. Someone said or someone thinks vaccines are harmful. It doesn't matter the kids will catch disease and could possibly become crippled or die. It doesn't matter all the scientific community has said there is no evidence the vaccines are harmful. The parents have anecdotal evidence and "honest opinions" from other parents to back up their view. It's sad but not changeable. People who are unaware of what is evidence and what is opinion have no way to make a rational judgment about their lives.

Learning was not the only activity we enjoyed. We made everything we did fun. Going places, singing, telling jokes, dancing, playing, and watching sports, and we love movies. We realized a few things about us that were different. For one thing none of us are shy. Even young students will challenge an idea they think is not clear.

Daniel said, "We are individually different and obviously have our own feelings about every subject. It is everyone's responsibility to look inside themselves and determine what they understand and what they do not understand." An inner understanding of all we study allows us to grow intellectually.

Being linked mentally gives us an advantage in everything we do. We can share what another person learns. Our being is a reflection of our feelings and there is no need to prove anything to others. We act with clarity of motive and never think something is foolish. Variation in views is a natural result of our individuality. We never criticize each other; we respect our differences. We do things most people are afraid of because we believe in ourselves. We have no shame or fear of criticism. It is natural to take chances with our social and intellectual lives.

We know when we are learning and love the feeling. We are aware it is very possible not to understand something. In some cases there could be various interpretations. We see variation in interpretations as a way of opening a subject to further examination.

We enjoy our parents and appreciate the support they give us. Our parents are always there for us and we realize their labor gives us the opportunities to grow and become our own future. We constantly tell each other how much we care for each other. We never loose a chance to demonstrate our feelings. We are very physical. It feels good to hug and kiss. Showing love for each other simply seems natural. We are really one big family, and growing.

Email to Washington:

This is really sickening to watch. The whole town walks around with smiles on their faces. They are playacting kindness to each other and even to strangers. There seems to be no conflicts between any of the parents and their kids. I mean none. They talk to each other and actually listen to each other. Who are they kidding? Only a group of aliens behave that way. Another thing, there is a great deal of promiscuity here, the way they are always hugging and kissing. I wouldn't mind hugging some of those bitches, but they overdo it. I really think these aliens are homosexuals. We see women holding hands and kissing each other; the males also hold hands, and when they meet, they kiss each other. It is really strange. We should place a fixed satellite over the village to record everything day and night. It may yield the proof we need. I'll keep you posted.

Our troubles hadn't disappeared. The government kept their eye on us, and we knew it. It was a game; when we spotted one of them, we waved. They were wasting a lot of time and money. We were no threat, but for some reason the government didn't know it.

Daniel said the government feared us and would eliminate us if they had a chance. They were just looking to find some excuse to attack us legally.

Our intellectual progress was incredible and rapid. We all applied to college, even though we were different ages, many, like myself, were quite young. While discussing our education, the subject of how to pay for it was raised. It was Vinny who suggested we study the economic system. His dad was an investment banker. So we spoke to Vinny's dad. Capitalism was egalitarian: it only required research, discipline, capital to invest, and patience.

Email from Washington:

No, we can't arrest them for being smart or gay. There must be some law they are breaking? Check the backgrounds of all the adults. We can use what we find to bring pressure on the group.

Email to Washington:

That kid, Daniel, has become their king. The whole town bows down to him. I told you he was the leader. He is the alien; probably his whole family are aliens. That Daniel, I'm sure, has taken control of all the minds of the people living in that town. That is the best explanation of the strange behavior. Why the hell would so many people follow a thirteen-year-old? I have friends in the press and will circulate our opinion that we think they are aliens, anonymously of course. Our best bet is to discredit them publicly, then, even if what we do is illegal, it will be accepted as done for the good of the country.

Daniel asked everyone to review investing and the capitalist model. There were many books and great information online. We interviewed a number of professional investors. We quickly realized most of them didn't have a clue. If they were successful, it was probably due to luck. Most stockbrokers only make money from buying and selling. They know very little about the stocks they trade. The most successful investors did well because they studied a narrow number of companies and knew a great deal about each.

In order to invest, we needed capital. We asked our parents to lend us the money explaining what we were going to do. There were questions, but in the end all the families pooled their money and we started to invest. They gave us $250,000 and wished us luck.

Email to Washington:

They are up to something. A lot of the families have given all their cash to that kid Daniel. We don't know yet what they plan to use the money for, probably to buy arms. The chatter we pick up is they want to invest the money in the stock market. Like these kids know what the hell they are doing? I can't imagine why all those adults would give their life savings to *a bunch of kids. Maybe the kids have some kind of a spell on the adults. We will watch closely. They have put together $250,000 in cash and are buying stocks. They are using that kid Vincent's father's firm to place the orders. I think this is a cover for whatever they are really doing. We can monitor the phones at the bank and can hear some of the bankers questioning the kids as to why they are buying certain stocks. They don't stop them. They just try to understand what they are up to. We have noticed that some of the brokers are investing their own money also. I'll keep you posted.*

We understood with money we would have many choices. We studied stocks, bonds, and real estate. Our parents were involved and worked with us. We enjoyed their input. Vinny's father was a great help. We used his company to do our investing. Sometimes he and his colleagues could not understand what we were doing, but they never interfered. They would ask for an explanation and let it go at that. But when we had great success, they joined us with their own money; they literally mirrored everything we did and enjoyed the same gains.

Our initial investment doubled in four months and then doubled again in two months. Within two years we were wealthy, with over five hundred million dollars. We would research and discuss then reinvest the money. We tried to know everything about each company. A couple of times we realized a company was in real trouble, so we shorted their stock and made money from their failure. The most important thing was the money bought us time. We knew we were safer with a lot of money. It may sound like a cliché, but money really does buy power.

The whole town became wealthy, not anything you could see. Almost no one bought a new car. We fixed our homes but very few bought new ones. The money was for education and helping others. We raised the town taxes, and 25 percent went to the town. It came off our federal taxes. With the tax money we built our own electric generator and generally improved the town. Best of all we hired better teachers, bought the best computers, rebuilt the school buildings with climate control. We opened our schools to any good student who wanted to attend. They were required to keep up their grades. Wealthy people have many political connections. So we contributed to all the politicians in the state of California. We backed many national senators in other states. In short, we bought protection, hired the best attorneys to defend us. At least until some of us graduated law school.

Within five years, we had more than a billion dollars. Daniel said that our success was because our research was pure, no egos, no one looking for recognition. Daniel insisted we pay all the required taxes being careful not to give the government any excuse to intervene in our lives.

Email to Washington:

We have found nothing to arrest them for; they don't even get traffic tickets. They have amassed over a billion dollars and counting. They must be cheating. Get the IRS and SEC to investigate maybe one of them can find something on them. I can't believe that with all our friends in high places you can't push someone to find something. They can make something up, and we can apologize later. At the least we may be able to get our hands on them and make sure they don't get away again. By the way, we should have invested in everything they did. We would be billionaires now.

—3—

REMEMBER THE SCENE IN the movie *Pretty Woman* when Julia Roberts retuned to the store that had refused to sell her clothes because of her appearance? In the scene, Julia Roberts, dressed in very expensive clothes, asked the clerk that refused to wait on her the day before, "You work on commission, right? Do you remember me? You refused to help me. Well, that was a big mistake, huge!" then she smiled and walked out.

More than once that happened to us. One of the earliest of those "mistakes" occurred when I was about twelve and Daniel was almost seventeen. Daniel, Sharon, Paige, and I went to LA to buy our mother a birthday present. The driver dropped us off on Rodeo Drive and waited with the car. We walked around trying to decide what to buy. We wandered into various stores, no one really paid any attention to us.

In this one jewelry store, we saw something we all thought would be perfect and asked the clerk if we could see the simple heart locket necklace.

The clerk looked at Daniel and asked, "Where are your parents?"

Daniel answered, "At home." We were then politely asked to leave. We looked at each other and just burst out laughing. So we went to another store. Almost the same thing happened.

Daniel said, "This is going to be harder than we figured." Each time we were refused service, we left. Some stores wouldn't even let us in. Daniel came up with a great idea. He approached a nicely dressed woman and asked if she didn't mind pretending she was our mother. Daniel even offered her a hundred dollars. He explained all she had to do was walk into the store with us and stand around and pretend we were together.

The first woman just looked at us and walked away asking, "Do you know who I am?" We actually tried to recruit two other women who looked at us as if we were sick. One thought we were part of a TV reality program.

After an hour of getting nowhere, hungry we walked over to the Beverly Wilshire Hotel, ordered lunch and laughed at the difficulties we were having just buying a gift. While eating, a discussion developed with two women on the next table. They asked lots of questions, where do you come from? How did we like LA? Where were our parents? How did we get here? When Sharon said we came by car and our driver was waiting for us, they got very interested. So I asked them if they would pretend to be our relatives so we could by our mother a present. Paige explained what had happened in the stores we visited. They were delighted to help us. After lunch we went back to the store where we had seen the heart locket.

It was so funny. As we walked in, the same salesperson who had asked us to leave ran over and welcomed us, paying complete attention to our escorts. We thought he would recognize us, but he didn't. We looked at the women. They realized from our looks that he was the jerk who had thrown us out. We walked over to an older female behind the counter asked if we could see the locket in the display case. She was very nice, and she took it out and we held it in our hand. Daniel asked how much did it cost? The price was four thousand dollars. She explained that it was platinum and was a signed piece from a famous designer. We were so pleased to have gotten service and able to get the locket we wanted. Daniel took out four thousand dollars in cash. Then Sharon said what about for my mother? And Paige said the same thing. So we wound up paying fifteen thousand dollars for three items. The clerk did a double take when we paid cash but and politely took the money. She was even nice enough to gift wrap them for us.

After leaving we thanked the two women. They said they had a great time just seeing the look on the face of that clerk when he realized who we were and we paid with cash. When we left the store, Daniel called for the car. We thanked the two ladies and handed them a thousand dollars each. They kept asking us who we were?

Daniel answered, "Just kids shopping for a gift, thanks again." Incidentally, my mother loved the locket.

Email to Washington:

We followed Daniel, his sister, and his girlfriend to Rodeo Drive in Beverly Hills. Do you believe they had a limousine and a driver pick them up in their town and drive them there, then wait for them for several hour? They ate lunch in the Beverly Wilshire Hotel where they were met by two women who accompanied them to a store. They went on a shopping spree, spending $15,000 in a jewelry store. We saw the two women receive a thousand dollars each from the kids as they were getting into the limousine. The women told us the most ridiculous story about just standing in the store pretending they were with the kids. We will follow up and see who the hell they are and what they were up to. We had to let them go. We could find nothing illegal about their actions. We are also checking out the store. It may be a front and they bought something as a coverup to a more nefarious scheme. Those scheming aliens. I couldn't believe the price of a lunch at the Beverly Wilshire Hotel. Have you ever eaten there? I'll keep you posted. See you next week in Washington.

In our early years we made a lot of money from interviews. The news media was so strange. Some reporters were very nice, but most had no respect for anyone, least of all us. The media wanted to interview "the space kids," especially Daniel, but really all of us who actually knew EL. They would beg for interviews. We had a press secretary who arranged the meetings, and collected the fees. The interviewers came from different sections of the media. Some were from major newspapers, others from science fiction journals. Many were just people with money who invited us to speak at their parties. We charged of course. We were paid fifty thousand dollars for an hour lecture, depending on how many of us attended. That is fifty thousand for each of us. If Daniel attended, it was automatically one hundred thousand dollars. We looked at it as only using the system to further our ends. We did visit public schools and shared our experiences with the children for free.

The lack of integrity of most reporters was disturbing. Very few were honest and actually listened, nor did they write what we said. Many times we would answer their questions and they would edit the answers to fit whatever angle they wanted. Many articles and shows were completely fabricated and had nothing to do with our answers. You would think that with all the video equipment, interviews would be on the up and up. But sadly no, they edited the data so it appeared we said something we didn't.

Daniel said reporters think all stories are about "them." They never examine the idea that is the story and what purpose it has. They ask questions and challenge people to show how clever they are." Very rarely do they look at the person they are interviewing and listen to the answers. They have an angle and their questions are geared to push the interviewee toward their angle. Daniel told one reporter "life is not about us; it is not about you or me, life is all about those we serve. We serve the universe of life; our responsibility is to humanity."

The reporter printed that Daniel said "our group serves the universe and our aim is humanity." This was "an admission that we are from outer space, and our target is humanity."

That certainly wasn't what Daniel said.

Email to Washington:

We have the media on our side. We give them anonymous scoops and they are thrilled to print whatever else we give them, no questions asked. Give them a few exclusive interviews with important people and they do as we direct. In a little while the public will understand how dangerous these kids are. I have gotten a few of the doctors from Hyde Park to confirm, off the record, that they believe these kids are not human. The stories discrediting Daniel are continuously coming out. I think we are making progress in turning public opinion against them. They are trying to pull the wool over the world's eyes with all the charity bullshit they do. But not for long. Almost every reporter can see they are hiding something. A few told me it is "creepy to sit down with them; they seem to anticipate the questions." Their answers are liberal trash about loving everyone and reaching out and helping. What nonsense.

Daniel had a strange experience with one reporter. The topic was world hunger. The reporter asked a question to which Daniel replied "our purpose is to serve the universe for the good of mankind." The reporter said you mean "your group serves the universe by controlling mankind?" Daniel said, "No, I didn't say that." The reporter then went on and on about what Daniel had said and the original topic never was discussed. Obviously, you can't have a serious discussion on a topic if what you say becomes the topic. So after that I became the spokesperson. I was already twelve years old.

Daniel didn't want to get involved with the nonsense anymore. He felt I was better equipped to deal with the reporters because of how I would burst out laughing when something silly was said. Daniel also said, in a very kind way, I was very aggressive and didn't tolerate nonsense.

The media is always claiming they are the protectors of democracy. They are, but it is purely accidental. There are very few Edward R. Morrows out there. Few reporters have a good understanding of their own motives and responsibilities. Fewer are willing to stand up for what is right at the expense of their salaries. Money and glory (scoops, exclusives) are most reporters' goals.

Anyway, there were whole programs about us and EL. The best one, of course, was the movie made by Stanley Stainer. But many were just geared to sell an angle. We had contacted EL and were working with the aliens. Some even said we were aliens. They had proof.

> *Email from Washington:*
>
> *Be sure to tune in tonight at 8:00 p.m. to Channel 4. We have sponsored a report to be aired which will give the public food for thought about whether these kids are aliens or not. We called in a lot of favors for this prime-time airing. It is really well done; wait till you see it. It cost a lot of money, but it's worth it. Some of those doctors from Hyde Park are appearing to explain their findings. They have agreed to clearly state their positions in exchange for protection against law suits for violating HIPPA laws. I'm trying to get the President to watch. He still doesn't accept our view that they are aliens. I don't push it with him. Eventually he will come around.*

A prime-time program beginning with a recapping of the story of the government capturing the alien in our home was aired. The reporter spoke of how we hid the alien and cared for it. The reporter dedicated at least five minutes to Daniel communicating with the alien through mental telepathy. They showed pictures of EL and then showed pictures of us speaking of how we had helped EL escape. How we brought EL to his spaceship so he could not be captured. The reporter asked, "How did the alien find its way to their house? Why their house? I ask you, if a creature as ugly as this one knocked on your door, would you let it in? Would anyone in their right mind just welcome and care for such a creature? This family not only welcomed it in their home, they fed it and helped it escape. And they communicated with it through telepathy. Can any of you out there communicate that way? No! Obviously these kids are aliens."

Further evidence of our being aliens was presented—"they are all intelligent beyond their age." The reporter said in a hushed tone, "When have you ever seen a whole town with so many advanced students? How can it be there are a thousand kids in one town all with IQs of 180 or better?" That reporter made up the number of kids and our IQs. There was no way of coming up with that figure.

As further proof the reporter had a video of us in school listening to our teachers. The reporter pointed out, in a hushed voice, "How is it possible all these kids are sitting there quietly and listening to the teacher?" Also, we were followed to the library and the reporter said, "What bunch of kids go on their own to the library? Are these really normal children? Look how strange they are. They are always polite. These kids hold hands. Not just male and female but also male and males. Also, you can see them kissing each other very passionately."

The reporter obviously believed that kissing was proof that we were aliens. The reporter said "Look at how young they are; this type of behavior is never seen in the normal population. Teenagers don't kiss like that." The reporter concluded the report with, "You can see in this town of excessively intelligent and polite kids, there are no real red-blooded Americans. These kids have to be aliens sent here to take over the world."

Email to Washington:

Great program last night. It really presented our point of view. It won't be long before the rest of the country understands what we are up against. Great job! I'm pushing some of the local media to follow up on the program. How did you get Dr. Herbert to go on the program? He clearly didn't believe the kids are aliens. He was our main obstacle while he was director of the project. Now he is on our side?

Email from Washington:

Great surprise seeing Dr. Herbert? It wasn't hard at all to get him to cooperate. We created a theft from his hospital and guess what, we had "proof" he did it? He had taken the money. There was nothing he could do, so we made a deal. No prosecution, we wipe the slate clean, and he stayed in his position. His being on the program added a higher level of credibility. He was actually glad he had presented his findings in public. Amazing! Or maybe it was the increased salary that helped.

There were nice stories too. Stories about how we loved EL and helped him because of that love. The best part was the media paid us a lot of money, which we invested. We didn't care what they wrote. At first it was disappointing. Daniel says the news media has an important role to play in preserving the rights of the individual within a culture.

Unfortunately, the role is accidental. The media prints a story. When interest develops, they run with it because it sells papers. Whether the story is true or not, does not matter. Within this formula they stumble upon their role as protectors of freedom. Particularly if the story revolves around politics. There is no real philosophy guiding them. Unless money is a philosophy?

Some stories were really aggressive. They wrote whatever would sell and didn't care if we got hurt. The news media incited groups to attack us and many "good Americans" called for the government to defend America against the aliens. There were demonstrations, marchers carrying American flags. But slowly this died down, and the media moved on to other threats to the American way of life and so did the groups that attacked us.

We decided we would buy one of the larger media companies to get our side of the story aired. We searched around for a company that dealt with all the media, TV, radio, web, and print and found one in financial trouble, bought it for one billion dollars.

Slowly, from behind the scenes, reporters who were clearly not interested in going after the facts were replaced. Usually they were busy inventing angles to create sensationalism where there was none. We hired a great liberal editor in chief. She hired young reporters who were less toxic and more open to the responsibility a journalist should have. The staff received great salaries and were provided with everything, cars, expense accounts, etc. We never got directly involved staying away from the operation of the company. It was a great success, though it slowly found itself being openly referred to by the government as a "pinko" paper. The reporters tried to hold a balanced opinion about any breaking news and always checked the sources.

Email from Washington:

_____

You were right, the evidence you brought me turned out to be very accurate. Those aliens actually own that pinko paper that attacks our elected officials. This information has brought us new allies. There are so many congressmen lining up on our side that I asked for an increase in our budget. We have received full support from Congress to do whatever is necessary to shut down that paper. The congress will protect us. I didn't tell the President because he would have objected. Be prepared to follow through with the plan you received the last time you were in Washington. Hold off for about two weeks while I milk Congress. This is going to be such fun silencing those left-wing bastards. There can be no trace to the government. We don't want the liberals having a new cause to march about. Also, we will probably get a reaction from the other news media companies. You know how protective of their own they are, so call in all favors. I'll do the same on this end. Remember to wait till I give you the go-ahead.

The company hired young people, some just out of college. Admittedly we placed some of our own interns within the organization, students from our journalism school. When other media would attack us for one thing or another, our company would insist on seeing the evidence. They did this with all stories not just the one's dealing with us. One main area of investigation was the political officeholders. Our paper turned up scandal after scandal.

The company developed a great following, most of our investment was returned in profits over the years. But, suddenly trouble began. At first companies pulled their advertising. Then a serious accident occurred at the warehouses of our main paper supplier. Two of their buildings in different states were destroyed. The company said they could no longer do business with our company. We told the CEO to offer to pay twice the going rate, but they refused. Then the FCC revoked the TV and radio licenses.

We kept everyone on payroll. They continued to do their job using the internet. Unfortunately, we had to close the company when the editor was killed and several reporters were beaten up. It was sad that these hardworking, honest people were hurt.

It was fairly obvious the government had a hand in the attacks. But there was nothing we could do. We provided all of our employees with five years salary and benefits. The editor's family was given a trust so her salary would be paid to her widower for the rest of his life.

One bitter note, none of the other news organizations, "the guardians of truth, justice, and the American way," even reported what was happening to their fellow journalists. They served the "truth" with silence. The death of our editor and chief, by an "unknown assailant" was only placed on the fourth page of almost all of the papers. On TV it was a ten-second filler, her picture and a mention that she died. Most of the reporters found jobs with other companies. Sadly, we could see, some had to change their philosophy.

Email from Washington:

Great job, all's well that ends well. There were a few eggs that had to be broken, but what the hell, we stopped them. Things got a little rough. Very few people actually got hurt. There is no loss getting rid of that editor. She would have gone on to some other paper with her bleeding heart. Those idiot kids arranged to have all the reporters kept on payroll. That's great for them. Now the reporters have learned to play in the big league, they will carry the lesson to future positions and won't be so eager to attack our elected officials. The good part is we have the complete trust of Congress. Actually, you could say, they are ours. They don't want to hear the details; they are impressed and relieved by the results. I thought that was a good touch having the newspaper building burned down after it closed. That will show those aliens that we are here. If they doubted our power, now they have something to think about.

—4—

B ECAUSE OF HOW QUICKLY WE LEARN, we were ready for college. I was already twelve. We applied to the best schools, and were invited to visit. They were curious to meet the "space kids." We made a big vacation out of the visits. Our parents came; we went sightseeing. We visited San Francisco, LA, Boston, Cuba, Hartford, Pittsburgh, Chicago, New York, Atlanta, Miami, Moscow, Beijing, Washington, DC, Houston, Cambridge, Oxford, Paris, Berlin, and many others universities. We were well treated because of our test scores and of course our money. Really, the money motivated our treatment and got us into the best schools. It was always the same: the president of whatever university would meet us with a committee of faculty members. They would bring some graduate students. We got a tour of the school, and then met privately with the chairman and faculty of various departments. We were looking for the best in our fields, so we often challenged them with questions. It was really nice to realize how little we really knew.

Email from Washington:

Can you believe those goddamn liberal colleges kissing the asses of those aliens? They are enrolling in the best schools in the world. Very smart of them. Then they will have real credentials to continue their effort to take over. They will come out of school and infiltrate our entire society. They may even move into government. For now, there is nothing we can do. But our turn will come. I have been assigned perma-

nently to this project, the gratitude of Congress. The entire operation is being taken below the radar. When the change of administration comes, they won't even know we exist. Our friends in Congress are afraid that the new president might object. He has been heard in the past praising those aliens for the good work they do. Congress will secretly fund our entire operation. Oh! Congratulations, you are now second in command. The raise will follow.

When a group of us were admitted to a school, we bought a house. It was easier. We like being together. In Boston, for example we bought a private estate. Also, near Stanford, Yale, and near Princeton we purchased very large estates. In New York City we bought three buildings one on Park Ave in the sixties, one near Wall St, and one near Columbia University. This was seen as protecting our group but also as a good investment.

We always studied as a group. At least ten of us in each school. That was also for protection. Mitchell and his friends went to MIT after Stanford. Daniel joined them and then I joined them at Harvard. Speaking of security, we had round-the-clock protection on our properties, surveillance as well as guards.

A funny thing happened to Daniel when he first arrived at MIT. He went online to see what properties were available near enough to MIT so we could walk to classes if we wanted. He found four places that seemed large enough to accommodate our group, so he made an appointment with the real estate agent of the property closest to MIT. In fact, it was located between MIT and Harvard.

Daniel arrived on time. As he walked in, the agent asked him what he was doing there. Daniel explained he had made the appointment.

The agent laughed and said, "What kind of a jerk are you, kid, to waste my time? How old are you anyway?" Daniel said seventeen. The agent loudly said, "Come back when your parents are interested."

Daniel didn't get annoyed. He smiled and asked if he could see the place anyway? The agent smiled and said, "Why not? I'm here." He said he was sorry to have called him a jerk. He explained he had driven an hour to be on time. That was why he had reacted so badly. Daniel could see he was a nice person who felt badly about the way he had spoken. They walked through the whole house, room by room. Daniel asked lots of question and enjoyed the tour. The place was on one acre. The main house was sixteen thousand square feet. There was a second small house, with four bedrooms on the other side of the garden. Daniel felt at home. He asked the agent, Douglas Smith, how much it cost?

Doug laughed and said, "For you, kid, it was only twenty-four million dollars." Daniel smiled and asked to go to the bathroom.

Once in the bathroom Daniel called one of our attorneys in Boston and asked her to bring everything necessary to purchase the property. The full price was twenty-four million dollars. He gave the attorney the address and asked how long would it take her to arrive? She said about an hour.

As Daniel came out of the bathroom with his cell phone in his hand, Doug jokingly asked, "Are your parents coming?" Daniel smiled and said they would be arriving within an hour. Rather skeptically Doug said, "Then we both should have a cup of tea." They were drinking the tea while Doug was giving Daniel advice about wasting people's time when the door bell rang.

Doug answered and sarcastically said to the very young attractive attorney, "You must be his mother?" The attorney ignored Doug and walked straight over to Daniel and said here are all the papers you requested.

"Thank you very much for rushing over. Please finish the purchase; I have to go to a class."

Doug was just standing there with his mouth open. Daniel turned to him and thanked him for being so nice and for the tour. As Daniel was leaving, he turned and said "my mother" will sign all the papers.

It is such a good story. We have had Daniel repeat it many times. I guess it is hard for some adults to see kids as people. Incidentally, Doug became our permanent real estate agent in the Boston area. We have since bought a few office buildings as investments. They were eventually deeded over to Harvard and MIT.

Email to Washington:

Those kids with all that money just bought an estate in Boston right near Harvard. My kid couldn't even get into Harvard. They get in and buy a mansion. If they had no money, no one would listen to them. See if we can cut off their wealth. They must have violated some laws to accumulate that much money so quickly. They just think they can buy their way into wherever they want to go. They travel all over the world and everyone just loves them. I don't know why the rest of the world does not see they are aliens. Is it only the two of us left out here to save humanity? I'm working on a few good media pieces and they won't be so high and mighty when they come out. I will forward you the reports when they are ready. Soon we'll change the world's view of them.

Email from Washington:

We have reports from all over the country they have purchased very large estates near the universities where students from their town are attending. Would you believe, in New York City they have acquired three large buildings: one by Columbia University, one on Park Avenue, near Hunter College, in the sixties, and one in the Village near NYU. I have every agency studying how they made the money. They can find nothing wrong or illegal. Those little bastards even paid all their taxes. What makes everything even harder is all those attorneys that work for them. But I'm sure we will find something to hang them with. You may be right about the two of us being the only ones that understand how dangerous they are. Even my friends here in Washington are laughing behind my back. They say I have created the threat. That it is a personal vendetta I have because the kid helped the alien escape from my unit. They just can't see how dangerous this

*"kid" is and all the followers he is gathering. But you just
wait; we'll show them.*

At college we were treated well. Some people could not accept such
young kids in college. Some of us were only twelve and thirteen years old
and looked like children. Eventually we were accepted as just another group
of freshmen. We interacted well with other students, making friends and
just enjoying ourselves. That doesn't mean we had no problems. Remember, there are always jerks around.

We all loved college with the parties and sports, especially baseball. We
could not understand the drinking and drugs. It was as if the students were
afraid of who they were and were trying to hide their personalities. Why they
thought an altered state would change who they were, we could not figure
out. After all, they were who they were, as we are who we are. Stranger were
those people who talked about reaching this or that level of understanding.
It was strange to us because as far as we could see, there is only one level—
the one you are at. You only have now and who you are now. You must learn
to enjoy who you are now, then the universe becomes visible.

Admittedly we are smart, and the work was interesting but not hard.
Daniel says "being smart is only a tool used to achieve your goals. Being
smart means we have a better chance to learn. It doesn't mean that we
know anything." We still had to study and try to understand. We all developed a clearer understanding of ourselves as we progressed. It was a wonderful time, so many things to learn. And when one of us understood, we
all understood. We realized we were different. We had become much more
intelligent. But more importantly, we shared our knowledge. We could tune
into each other's feelings and share our experiences. We were particularly
pleased with the professors who enjoyed what they were doing. They really
added to our lives and knowledge.

Our original group all went to MIT, and Harvard. That was Daniel's
idea. He felt we would do better if we helped each other, and were physically close. Whatever parents wanted to come were welcomed. Some enrolled in courses. Oh, of course my mother came. She also got engaged to

Kiel, so we saw him all the time. At first, we thought he was spying, but they were happy together, and we were happy for them. He was forced to retire, accused of not being objective when it came to our group. He was "too involved" with us.

Everyone found girlfriends and boyfriends. Daniel had Paige. I wasn't allowed to date. Ma said not to worry; I would be okay. And I knew it was important to enjoy each stage of life and not rush it. I felt the desire to be with Vinny and he with me, but there was so much I had to learn about my body.

It was a real shock when I developed breasts. Granted I was hoping for them, and when they came, they weren't that big. But it was strange, in a nice way, and at the same time I was proud and ashamed. The real shock was when I got my period. It threw off my thinking and feelings. I had to take time to understand and feel this new person I had become.

I told Daniel about my confusion. He said, "the menstruation was the woman's mark of maturity. This event brings them to examine their bodies better. The strangeness is the catalyst to thought. Every month renews the question of 'who am I?' Men have no marker to maturity that is why they don't mature as early as women. Men have no monthly reminder; this limits their development."

In the summers, we traveled all over the world. Meeting people in other countries was exciting, better than the books. We fit right in. Our money allowed us many advantages. We could travel as we pleased and were well protected. Before visiting, we read about the place, reviewed their culture and language. You should have seen the faces of the people wherever we went when they realized we could speak their language.

Most places heard of the "space kids" and were curious to meet us. We were invited to speak at local schools and meet the students. They asked about EL and his spaceship. Only once in a while were we asked if it was true that we were aliens. This interacting with the kids made our vacations wonderful. They were so surprised to see how young some of us were. There was a spiritual connection in many places. Some people we knew before we were formally introduced. It was as if we had shared our lives together at some point.

Wherever we went, we set up programs to assist in the education of the children and developed health care where it was lacking. Foundations were set up to fund the schools and hospitals. We invested in water projects bringing fresh water to villages, farming coops, with education to introducing cash crops to the local farmers.

On one of these trips, Daniel was asked what did he mean when he spoke of sharing the universe?

He responded, "We all have moments when we feel the world around us in a way that fills us with the joy of the moment. Some people call it a state of grace. You feel complete and all around you becomes part of you. All those with you become the meaning of love. The love you feel is a reflection of the joy of being and you know you are privileged to share with another person, a tree, a sunset, or just a moment. A moment when you become universal and you are a dream in the universe. I have experienced that feeling from time to time. Not often, but enough to make me feel privileged to be a part of the universe."

Email from Washington:

These kids are flying all over the world recruiting sympathy and followers wherever they go. They apparently can speak almost every language. Now that's not normal. But I have not been able to get the President to accept that action must be taken soon before they become too powerful. At least I'm on the inside. They just don't see what you and I have realized from the beginning. I push the issue at every meeting. It has become a standing joke, but as soon as we have proof, they will come around. I do have a number of congressmen who are on our side. They have even tried to pass legislation that would give us access to the aliens' books, but they are still in the minority, the rest will come around soon. We have good support at the Pentagon, but without the President's OK, they can do nothing. Our day will come.

One night, it was actually a beautiful night, I remember it very clearly, like it was yesterday, I probably will never forget it. I stayed late at the Harvard library. I would almost never be alone. But this night everyone had someplace to be, and I didn't want to stop what I was doing. Besides, I loved the walk to our house. The grounds of Harvard are beautiful with gardens and trees. Our estate wasn't far, just outside the Harvard gates. The moon was out, and I was thinking how nice it was to just walk and enjoy nature. Also, to be all alone was something that almost never happens and it felt good. I was walking along quietly and began to sense the presence of someone else, but I ignored the possibility I was being followed. The night was so beautiful and I was preoccupied so I didn't pay much attention. I was still on the college grounds and felt safe. I thought it might be one of those government jerks who were always following us.

Suddenly I was attacked by this very big man who grabbed me from behind. He started punching me in the head and I felt dizzy. He didn't say a word, just kept hitting me. I was shocked he threw me on the ground touching me and grabbing me. I was so scared I didn't know what to do. It sounds dumb, but it all happened so fast that I panicked and felt lost and hurt and everything was pushed together in my head.

Once he had me on the ground, he ripped off my skirt and my underpants and then he was about to take down his pants when, suddenly, from deep inside me came a scream. The scream was so shrill that I felt it was like a knife being thrown at my attacker. I had never done that before. It was so strange because as soon as I screamed the man went flying, thrown against a tree. He was lying there twisted unable to move. His whole body appeared to be broken bleeding badly.

I immediately covered up, putting on my skirt and while crying I dialed 911 on my cell phone. I sat there till the police arrived. They came quickly and so did our whole group. The police were very understanding. I felt safe.

One of the officers calmly spoke to me. At first, I couldn't understand what she was saying, but slowly I became aware of my surroundings and understood the questions. The police called for two ambulances and interviewed me while we waited. The man was badly hurt. The EMTs immediately started working on him. They were trying to stop the bleeding while placing him in an ambulance. I, too, was taken to the hospital. The nice police officer and my mother rode with me. On arrival I was examined by a doctor. I had minor cuts on my head and neck, and a black eye. What was worst was that I felt scared and ashamed.

The police took my statement. I told them what I remembered and how I felt. I left out the part about my scream. They were very kind. A female officer did the interview. She said the man had been convicted of a previous assault on a young girl, in fact, he was out on parole. It appeared to her from the evidence, and what I said, that when he got up to expose himself he must have tripped and hit his head on the tree. The doctors could not save him, a number of organs were punctured.

She felt I was very lucky because he was such a big man I could have been seriously injured. She said who knows what he might have done? He might have "killed you." This was the first time I was exposed to violence. Nor did I ever consider the possibility I could be killed. I guess no fourteen-year-old does. It was good Daniel and the gang were with me. It was a great comfort to have my brothers and friends there. Oh! Also my mother, of course, I milked that.

Finally, the doctors said I could leave. My mother and I signed some papers, and I went back to our house. We had messages on our phones and emails from everyone. They all felt the attack. Back in our house we relaxed and sat down to discuss what had happened.

Daniel was most interested in how I screamed and the attacker was thrown by an obvious amount of force. While we were discussing it, Daniel recalled how EL screamed once when we scared him and things went flying. Apparently, I had that ability. Each of us tried to duplicate the scream, but it quickly became apparent it only happens when we are really scared. It must have looked funny to see a whole house full of adults and kids walking around screaming. This attack, however, exposed a problem, we were vulnerable and could easily be physically attacked. We needed a way of protecting ourselves.

Email to Washington:

Daniel's sister, Kate, claimed she was attacked by a sex pred-ator. We are unable to understand how she survived. She got a black eye, but otherwise she was totally unharmed. She did manage to kill a very large man. His body was completely broken internally. Remember Kate is only fourteen and can't weight more than 125 pounds. Our man following her said it all unfolded very fast. The attacker had her naked and was about to enjoy the moment when she suddenly screamed and the man went flying. I tell you these kids have enormous power. The attacker's body was completely destroyed inter-nally. The doctors had no way to save him and had no expla-nation of how he sustained his injuries. I have ordered new equipment to allow us to follow them more closely. If we can get on video them using their powers, you could use it to con-vince the cabinet to go along with stronger measures.

Email to Washington continued:

We have a copy of the police report and I have spoken to the officers that were present, only the female officers got an-noyed when I tried to suggest there was more to the story. The others felt that Kate was hiding something. There is no mention of the scream our guy heard in the report. Who knows how she did it? I don't think she was just lucky? That scream may have been the sound of an offensive weapon? She might have blown him away with it? It's too bad the guy didn't kill the bitch! A complete report will follow.

Our protection became our number one priority. We would invest in creating an electronic shield. Only our own engineers would work on it to prevent anyone outside our group from learning whatever operating mode it would have. Very quickly, within a few weeks, they came up with a force field to protect us. They eventually got it to shield our cars as well as our homes and all the surrounding grounds. The entire system was perfected to where we eventually protected our entire town.

But before we had the protection of the shield, we decided no one should go out alone. We walked in groups everywhere. We hired more protection details from a security company. They watched our homes and also provided armed escorts.

<hr>

Email to Washington:

They are on to us. In the last week they have hired a great deal of protection as well as installing protective devices. I am contacting the agency they contracted with, as well as the workers, so we can get eyes inside. This may work out to get us the proof we need. There are a few classmates that consider the whole group strange. They just can't put their finger on what they feel. One student swears they share thoughts. He said that one of "them" checked out a new physics book on Monday. This is a large complicated book with 400 pages. The book was returned on Wednesday. He could hear all of "them" discussing the book on Friday. They were referring to chapters and pages. You can understand that if they can learn and quickly share information, in a very short time they will master all human culture. Then we are doomed unless we do something. It is a good thing we have our team in place. We just need proof to get the go-ahead from the upper ups. I was thinking I'd like to get my hands on that Kate. I'll teach her a thing or two. Who knows what power she used to kill that poor fellow?

After the attack I started practicing ways to protect myself. I used my mind to move objects. I had a little success, small things, but it was a start, I hoped to get better. I practiced all the time. I had gotten to the point where I could easily just look at something, a small object like a pencil, and move it at will. I was proud of my progress but didn't tell anyone. I was saving my successes for when I could control big objects and really wow them.

They say lightening never strikes twice, but it did. I was majoring in advanced math, while I was loved by the professors, there was a group of students on my case all the time, just obnoxious. I went about my days enjoying college and ignoring the "jerks."

One night I had been invited to a party. I was greeted warmly, had a ginger ale and even was asked to dance, which I enjoyed. It made me feel older, more grown-up. When I went onto the patio, there were four of my classmates who were always teasing me. They said things like "does your mother know you're out late," they called me "pimple face." They were out for fun in the way intoxication makes popular, and kept encouraging each other to be bolder and more aggressive. I figured if I ignored them, they would go away.

At first one of them simply tried to hit on me saying things like "you're so attractive why waste it all on schoolwork?" I didn't respond I figured silence was a good defense. Then he got nasty saying "what good is smart if you've never been kissed." I decided to go back inside, as I turned away one of the jerks started cursing saying "let's teach this bitch a lesson." I turned back to look at them and saw one of them moving to hit me. Angrily I stared at him and with my mind I threw him into the bushes. To my surprise it worked then I did the same with the second attacker. The other two ran away. I was a little shocked it worked so well and how easy it was. I was also very proud of my achievement.

A number of guests came running and called the police. When the police arrived, the boys said I beat them up for no reason; "she threw us with her eyes." There were plenty of witnesses who said the boys tried to hit me. They all described what they saw but could not explain how I had defended myself. Some of the witnesses said I used judo. The police laughed at the jerks who were screaming I had beat them up. They kept repeating "she threw us with her eyes." The police laughed when they gave the names of the boys who had run away, as their witnesses. The police weren't buying their story since it was obvious they were drunk.

One cop said, "So your story is this little girl, who doesn't have a mark on her, beat up four of you."

I told the police I didn't want to press charges so long as they didn't bother me again. Some of our group saw me throw the jerks. They were very surprised and excited, looking forward to examining my method. The outsiders who saw it just kept repeating I had used some kind of martial art like judo on the guys. I was so very proud of myself.

Email to Washington:

I tell you they have powers that are not human. That same little bitch, Kate, Daniel's fourteen-year-old sister, almost killed a group of innocent guys. This time it was four twenty-year-old math students who were at a party enjoying themselves. All the witness say that Kate got angry with them and threw them in the air like they were paper dolls. All the witnesses agree that the guys approached her and in a fit of anger she simply threw them. Some were thrown for a distance of ten feet. Can you imagine how nasty she is to have hurt those guys just because she refused their advances? I have never liked her. She's the kid that wanted a bed for her doll at Hyde Park. She has a big mouth and is aggressive as hell.

Email to Washington continued:

Actually, there is something sexy about her, and guys will be guys. She's the type you have to tie up and train. But if she has the ability to hurt people with her eyes, we should just kill her before she gets us. That is probably how she killed that other poor chap. We are going to see if the location has surveillance video. Maybe someone at the house used their phone to take a video. I will follow it up. We are getting closer to having the proof we need to get the cabinet to listen to you.

The next morning, we gathered to discuss this apparent new power. After a good breakfast I explained exactly what happened and how I had been practicing moving objects. Everyone was very interested. No one had used their mind to move objects, let alone to attack another person. It was a controlled attack, but this was a new power that we had to explore.

As I told the story, everyone tuned in to my thoughts and feelings. They could feel the energy I created to throw the jerks and where the energy came from. After they had a good understanding of how it was done, we picked a statue in the garden and decided to practice. We all concentrated using the method. It was so scary because the statue didn't go flying, it disintegrated. Apparently, we overdid it (smile). We spent the entire day working to control the power to prevent injuring anyone.

We found this was a great new discovery and, like the children we were, it was so much fun. We were marching around moving objects. We hoped no one could see us laughing and playing with our new toy. At supper we were still playing. It was fun to have our vegetables raise up and come to our plates. But the greatest fun came with dessert when Daniel made a little speech thanking me for the discovery and then flung Jell-O into my face. Immediately, of course, we all threw Jell-O. What a mess, but it was well worth it.

We continued the next day experimenting and having fun. Then I did something that changed the ball game. While looking at Mitchell I thought it would be fun to see if I could force his eyes to close, like a blink that doesn't open. The problem was that it worked and Mitch went into a panic, quickly I stopped. But this was the beginning of an entirely new line of research. We would now concentrate on bodily functions. We really had to be careful; we didn't want to stop someone's heart.

While cleaning up the mess, Gary cut his finger. Jokingly I looked at it and to our surprise it began to heal. So we spent the entire next day working on that. We were so happy to have spent time together. And, of course, we had much to teach the others when we returned home. More importantly we knew we could protect ourselves if we were attacked. It made our college days easier.

Email to Washington:

We have first-hand testimony from the guards that protect

their Harvard estate. They didn't actually see how the kids did it, but two of the guards said that very large statue was turned to dust over night. The cleaning staff also reported food thrown all over the dining room. There was a large amount of Jell-O on their clothing in the wash. We are getting closer; they must be practicing something. I believe it is related to the incident were that Kate threw those four innocent guys. Whatever happened to the investigations by Home Land Security and the IRS into these aliens? Someone should turn up something. By the way, we have been unable to monitor their phones or get ears in their property. Our engineers think they have a jamming device. There is also some kind of a force field protecting them. They have no guards inside their property and the guards outside say that it is not possible to enter the property at all without an escort.

Email to Washington continued:
_____
They are describing an invisible wall around them and their property. If that is true, imagine the military applications. We could march our army into any country in the world and they could do nothing to stop us. Try speaking to some of the top brass at the Pentagon. I bet they would be very interested in getting their hands on this; we can plainly see they are getting more powerful. We have to kill them all soon before it is too late. Just give me the word and I'll take the rap if necessary.

Email from Washington:
_____
The IRS is very close to building a case against them. Then we can arrest them and put them away. Once they are in custody this time, they won't get out. We really think if we can lock up Daniel and his sister Kate, we can bring the others down. It may be that Daniel's family are the aliens and they

control the others. Soon we will get our hands on them. We have constructed an electronic jail that prevents energy from being transmitted. As soon as we have them in custody, we will begin our interrogation. We have the green light to do whatever is necessary to extract their secrets. Can you imagine the weapons we would have at our disposal? Who knows, we may be able to take over the world for ourselves. With their powers the United States would be supreme. We will get them and wring the secrets out of them. But one thing is for sure, they will never leave our custody alive again.

Email to Washington:

I'm glad there is to be an initiative. I'm ready. Once we have them, I want that Kate. I know she's young, but she is the real bitch that must be tamed, and I know just how to do it. I agree, once we have them, we get what we want, and then kill them. It will be an absolute pleasure to destroy that whole town. We will also get hold of all that money they have. The main thing is to force them to give us the secrets they have to that force field and whatever device creates that scream that kills people. My team is so ready to move, finally.

Being together made the college experience great. Learning new ideas and having so many people interested in learning was a true mind opener. We particularly loved being with the professors who were so knowledgeable and willing to share their ideas. It is a wonderful moment when you realize you understand something. A true joy to feel the love when an idea becomes yours. The joy similar to finding the right phrase or a line in a poem that remains for you a moment of love and understanding, e.g.; "do not go gentle into the good night," cowards die many times before their death, the valiant never taste of death but once," "home is where when you go there, they have to take you in," "being lied about don't deal in lies," there are so many others that become part of who you are. Our time in college went quickly; then we went on to various graduate programs, e.g., law school, advanced physics, almost every field you can think of.

Our research in our various fields yielded many inventions that we patented and sold. We invented a way to transmit electricity without wires. Daniel said we didn't really invent it, a man named Nikola Tesla did in the early twentieth century, but no one ever figured out how he did it. We sold the patent for 10 billion dollars.

After college we set up companies so we could work together. Not all in one company but many different businesses. We set up charities and hired our relatives to work and collect salaries. That is how rich people employ their kids. We were always careful about paying taxes. We had our own attorneys and accountants. Oh, our original group moved back to our home in California. By now we were worth about eighty billion dollars. But the money was a mixed blessing. True we had unlimited choices, but we also came under close scrutiny of the IRS.

We were constantly in the spotlight with many people contacting us asking for money or to invest in their ideas. Business magazines printed stories about our wealth. These were positive stories which we felt encouraged others to reach their possibilities.

Email from Washington:

I have convinced a few congressmen that something has to be done. They don't like the President anyway, so it is an opportunity to show how indecisive he is. They assured me my name would not come up, and they will move soon to bring this Daniel to answer for his arrogance. This, at the least, will bring public attention to what we have realized all along is a very serious situation. Hopefully, after the hearing I can get the go-ahead to attack them. Just have all ready. There may be some light at the end of this tunnel after all.

One day Daniel was called to testify before the Senate Housing Committee; he went with a few of our lawyers and my future husband Vinny, who is our chief investment officer and Mitchell's wife Ebana who is our chief financial officer. After he was sworn in, the chairman thanked him for coming to which Daniel responded that it was his honor.

"I always wanted to visit the Capital. This is truly a unique way to see congress in action." There were a few laughs but immediately the mood changed. The chairman went into a long speech about how Daniel and his companies are undermining the American way of life. The fact that Daniel provided health care to all employees was applaudable but giving all employees five weeks vacations was "absurd." The senator went on and on about the excessively higher wages we paid our employees. And how our companies paid all the educational expenses of the employees and their family members. Though this seems like something to be praised, he said it was really "anti-labor."

Then he launched into a sermon on how the low-cost housing we provide our workers was an attack on the real estate market, which we were destroying. He even suggested we were hoping to capitalize on the future collapse of the real estate market. He had evidence that we were shorting REITs.

The senator paused and asked Daniel what did he have to say about that?

Daniel responded by asking, "About what?"

The chairperson then became angry and hollered, "About you destroying the housing market."

Daniel responded, "Providing good housing for employees is good business. There is no evidence the practice in any way effects the housing market." The chairperson got even angrier and said he had proof showing Daniel's statement was wrong, and he could see Daniel was not cooperating with the committee.

He asked Daniel, "do you have anything to add to your response?"

Daniel then went into a discussion of the real estate market and the current prices in various locations in the US. He pointed out the few million low-cost homes provided had no effect on the market. Daniel said, "As to the five weeks paid vacation for all our employees, that is what all workers in Europe receive. Why shouldn't American workers receive the same?"

Daniel pointed out even with all the costs of providing these benefits, his companies still made billions of dollars in profit. "Obviously the senator could clearly see, from our high profits and low turnover of employees, it is sound economic policy, to take of care employees." He pointed out "workers are the most important part of any company; not to take care of them was just absurd. Looking out for their health, their families and their future is good business and morally responsible capitalism."

Another senator on the committee jumped in and said, "Are you calling the chairperson a liar?" One of our attorneys spoke with Daniel. Daniel then looked at the committee and said he was not calling anyone a liar; the committee had not been provided with correct information. "If the committee would allow, the correct data can be uploaded to your computers within a few minutes."

The chairman went into a rage screaming at Daniel, "HOW OLD ARE YOU?"

Daniel responded, "Twenty-two."

The chairman got even angrier and screamed, "WHO DO YOU THINK YOU ARE, YOU LITTLE ARROGANT SON OF A BITCH?"

Daniel sat there consulting with our attorneys while the senator called Daniel every curse in the dictionary.

Ebana told Daniel, "It would be best if we just leave." So they stood up and walked out while the chairman kept banging his gavel and screaming "you come back here; you have not been dismissed." They just walked out without looking back. Vinny later told me the story. He felt the senators had only one reason to call Daniel to the committee, to humiliate him.

The news media was all over the story. There were no actual facts printed. No mention of how Daniel was attacked for providing a decent environment for workers. There was no mention of how Daniel politely tried to answer the questions. There was also no mention of the senator calling Daniel a "son of a bitch." The stories were all about how arrogant Daniel and his group were and how Daniel had "called the senators liars" and just got up and left while the senators were talking to him. That was their story, even though the reporters were present in the hearings and it was captured on video.

Their headline read "Arrogant alien calls US senators liars."

Email to Washington:
_____

That was great. Now the truth is coming out. People are seeing Daniel and his family for what they are. We have to convince the general public they aren't just arrogant, but also a danger to our planet. If we can get our hands on one or two of them and run our own DNA tests, we can prove our case. If we get our hands on one of their women (hopefully that murderer Kate), I would really like to do the interrogation. I'm sure I can get her to talk, and in the process, I'll show her what a real man is like. She really is annoying with her lack of fear of any of us. She is the one, I'm sure that inspires all those rescues around the world. We must keep up the pressure. I'm going to try to provoke Daniel in hopes they will use their powers and we can capture it on video. Once we show the American public what they can do, they will realize they are not just adorable, lovable kids. Hopefully they will come to understand what we have been saying, they are not human.

It didn't stop there. A week after the Senate fiasco, the government came after us. While Daniel was on a business trip to New York, he was served with an arrest warrant stating he owed back taxes. Obviously, the Senate had called their buddies at IRS. They were going to even the score. The cops went to grab Daniel; the force field prevented them from touching him. They tried over and over again with the same results. The cops drew their guns. Daniel told them to calm down; he would accompany them. So, they walked to the police station. At the police station the police tried to put Daniel in a cell, but he refused to be locked up. They got agitated and our attorneys calmed everyone down. They took Daniel before a judge. The district attorney said Daniel was a flight risk. He cited Daniel's wealth and the fact he owned his own planes making it easy for Daniel to leave the country. The judge set bail at one billion dollars. We quickly posted it.

Daniel was very upset and he said so.

"We should not allow the government to place us in a situation where a lack of freedom would allow them to experiment. We should use every power we have to prevent it from happening." He looked at me and said, "Sis, you know exactly what you would have to do if the situation ever arose." I just smiled. Our attorneys pushed to get a trial date. When the date arrived, the government asked for a postponement. This went on for two years. The trial was set for June, three months away, the government asked again for a postponement. This time the judge did not allow their request.

Email to Washington:

How the hell did Daniel slip through our fingers? This was our opportunity to dissect him. What happened? Who the hell was that judge that let him out on bail? We finally had him and a stupid judge just let him get away. That is the problem in America today. Too many lawyers, too many judges. They seem to think the law is more important than our survival. At every turn there is a bleeding heart from the ACLU serving papers to get traitors off. Why should there have to be a trial? Just shoot them. Fortunately for our country, you and I can see clearly what those aliens are up to. It is a damn shame all those bleeding hearts insist on there being proof before they will take action. Can't they see they have those powers that prevent us from even touching them? That's not proof?

Email from Washington:

I can see you are very upset. Believe me so am I. We just couldn't believe it; he is untouchable. They really did try to take him into custody, but there was no way to even touch him. Without exaggerating, the police were unable to lay their hands on him let alone cuff him. They really do have special powers. Fortunately, it was all caught on video and we can use it to our advantage. It has already gone viral.

This is what we have been saying all along. Finally, now they can see it for themselves. It has to be obvious to anyone seeing the video that Daniel is not human. I will push ahead with my request to the cabinet to allow an attack on them physically. In the mean time we will keep up the media pressure. Do what you can at your end. Be ready with your team, we are close to getting the green light to attack.

When the trial finally did begin, we represented ourselves. The government wouldn't explain how much he owed. They kept referring to income that was not reported to IRS, which our attorneys demonstrated had been accounted for in our tax returns. There were questions that had nothing to do with taxes. Our attorneys kept objecting and the judge, fortunately, sustained their objections. Finally, our attorney asked the judge to have the government state the amount they thought Daniel owed and on what evidence? The judge was very fair, he even got annoyed at the government's attorneys. He felt their case was weak and said so.

After a few weeks, the government came up with a ridicules sum. They said we owed four billion dollars. The judge was even more annoyed. He said from what he reviewed that was excessive. The government had exaggerated their claim. The judge was impressed with all the charities we supported and said so. He said there was no proof of criminal intent. He allowed a fine of two hundred million dollars based on a technicality. There had been some international taxes with no clear way of being reported. We had listed the taxes based on an IRS ruling, but there was another formula the government used to show we owed back taxes.

Boy, were the government attorneys surprised when our attorney wrote a check there in the court room for the entire amount. The judge took the check and closed the case. The government uses the IRS to threaten people. If they find nothing, they don't even apologize, even though it might have cost a person a fortune to defend themselves. If the government could have convicted Daniel, they would have tried to send him to prison. We were lucky to get an honest judge who looked at the facts and refused to rubber stamp the government's case. We would never allow any of us to be detained. If they wanted us, they would have to come get us. We knew, at least for now, they couldn't touch us.

Email to Washington:

That's what's wrong with the judges in our country, they think that the law is above national security. You should have threatened that bastard before he made a decision. Who appointed him? I've said it before and I'll say it again, these liberal judges over intellectualizing everything. They think that the law actually matters. Why can't they understand that our country comes first? He let another opportunity slip through our hands. Why don't we just take actions on our own? These traitor judges always think they are upholding "the law." You give me the word and I can mobilize a special unit to defend our way of life. Maybe we should get rid of some of those liberal judges? There would be a little noise for a while. We can pin it on some radical group. They are dumb enough to take the credit or deny it in a way that no one believes them. The more I think about it the better it sounds. What do you think?

We were living all over the world running various businesses and charities. Our original group from the hospital decided to move back to our homes in California. We would be better protected in our town. There was no problem running our business from there; we had computers and many of the companies ran on their own. Back home together we would be better able to protect ourselves.

Once home, we bought all the surrounding land ten miles in all directions from the center of town. We paid for every home and all the land. One farmer, whose property was worth about two million dollars on the open market, held out until we paid him twenty million. All structures outside of five miles from the center of town were demolished. We closed our town to outsiders.

Email to Washington:

They are making their move. They have bought up all the land around their town for ten miles in every direction. We can see them strengthening their positions. They are erecting fortifications and installing electronic equipment. They have created a barrier of open land five miles in all directions, a no-man's land that is probably where their spaceships will land. They have set up check points and have restricted entry into their town. They have their own police. I tell you they are getting ready to attack us. They have enormous storage capacity, and with their wealth they might even buy an atomic bomb.

Because of the threat from the government, we used various methods to prevent our money being traced. We bought companies all over the world, diverse companies, with no connection to us. The town's operating budget and pension fund held a lot of our stock. We had numerous secret deposits.

Back home we were so happy. Mitch and a few others were married. Daniel was engaged to Paige with their wedding day picked. We liked weddings. The entire town participated. A wedding is a great occasion for a party.

I was sneaking around with Vinny. I knew he was older, but we really got along well. We didn't have sex or anything. Well, we did kiss and hold hands. I was learning to deal with those feelings. Teenagers have many problems, even ours. They have to learn about relationships. They get along, but have to learn about sexual elements. Not about sex, that's easy, they know how. What they have to learn is intimacy. They have to learn to appreciate the feelings of their partner. Even though they can tune in to each other's feelings, it takes time to evaluate the emotional experience and overcome the confusion it creates.

Originally our town had about 2500 people. But more and more people joined us. We could tell if they belonged. We, the original group, could see their thoughts. So, we knew if they would fit or not. We employed any town member who needed work. If you walked down our main street, it looked like any other with stores, car repair shops, two movie houses, a theater, etc. The town was powered by solar energy and fuel cells. There was no garbage to be buried nor burned. Everything was recycled even the table waste we used as compost.

Quickly we rerouted the highway that originally went through our town and turned the old highway into a private road. At first there was government objection, but we paid for it ourselves and with all our money and lawyers the government quickly realized they could do very little to stop us. Also, the large amount of money we contributed to our state politicians helped. We built our own airport. We built a section of warehouses to hold a large quantity of supplies in case we might need them. These buildings would come in handy. The news media said we were paranoid. We felt we had good reason.

Daniel went to work to develop our land to produce fruits and vegetables we might need. We had lots of land, and with the right equipment we would soon have good farms. These would be used to teach agriculture in our schools. In setting the farms up we had a very funny incident.

Email to Washington:

We have been unable to bring any pressure on them from the state authorities. They have bought all the politicians. They have also bought all the labor unions and police departments. They actually contributed one hundred million dollars to the Police Benevolent Association. With their kind of money, they are untouchable. Our only hope is to knock them out with force. See what you can do, or, just give me the word. We are ready. They continue to reinforce the town as a fortress. It is next to impossible to actually see the town from the perimeter. There is no way to get any closer than ten miles. We use high-definition cameras and access the satellites to keep watch. Whatever happened to my request that we place a stationary satellite above their town?

—5—

AFTER LEAVING THE HOSPITAL and going back to school, we saw ourselves as "normal people." Even after we made a lot of money, we still didn't see ourselves as anything special. We knew we were intelligent and had certain abilities, but still we tried to just live what we considered "normal lives." To avoid being the objects of curiosity, many times we went far from our town where there was no media to bother us. But even when we went thousands of miles away, we sometimes found ourselves in funny situations.

Daniel has this fascination for gadgets. Often, he would send for items in catalogs. He once bought a robotic vacuum cleaner that ate one of his rugs. Daniel told Paige it was hungry.

One day, Daniel decided to go to a farm equipment fair in rural Ohio. Paige, my sister Sharon, and I went with him. We had arranged for a car and driver to meet us at the airport. The fair was about ten miles from the airport, and we enjoyed seeing all the farms and flat land in Ohio. It was very different than the California landscape. We didn't feel out of place; there were a lot of other young adults at the fair. We went on rides, loved the bumper cars. We ate hot dogs and popcorn. We had a great time.

At each booth Daniel would ask a lot of questions. Most salespersons would answer one or two, then they would get a little annoyed and tell us to come back with our parents. It didn't stop Daniel. Then we came upon this one salesperson who was really engaging. He offered us something to drink. We sat there with him while he told us about his family. He actually answered every question and, where he could, he showed us the item on his computer. Sometimes he excused himself to speak to other customers. We just waited till he came back. He always apologized for the interruption. We really liked him.

After three hours of questions and answers, and Daniel examining each item, Daniel told the man he was ready to place an order. The salesperson, Ron Talbot, asked Daniel what he would like? Daniel answered, "Everything you have, but I need six of these and four of this," and finally after going over the list, Daniel smiled and said, "Double the order."

Ron said okay and made out an invoice, turning to Daniel, he said, "It came to $6,120,000." Daniel pulled out a checkbook and wrote a check for the full amount. Daniel asked did that include shipping and handling? Ron said yes. Daniel wrote out our address and asked how long before delivery? Ron said about thirty days.

Daniel shook Ron's hand and thanked him very much. Ron smiled from ear to ear and said, "Kid, you really play a good role. I have kids at home, but you are really very convincing. Thanks for the order." Daniel said you're welcome and again asked how long before we receive the equipment? Ron said after the check cleared it would take about thirty days. Daniel said fine, thanking him again.

Two months went by and we hadn't received the delivery, Daniel called Ron and told him we hadn't received the equipment, and asked when would it arrive? Daniel pointed out that the check had not yet cleared the bank.

Ron responded, "Kid, when you play a game, you go all the way."

Daniel just cracked up laughing, then told Ron, "Listen, Ron, I need the equipment for our farm. Just give me the benefit of the doubt and deposit the check. If the check doesn't clear, don't send the equipment. If it does, please fill the order and have it here in thirty days like you promised." Ron was laughing on the phone and told Daniel he had told his family and friends about how serious he was.

Daniel raised his voice and said, "Stop laughing and deposit the check, I need the equipment." Daniel then hung up.

A week later we got a call from Ron; he was beside himself apologizing, saying how sorry he was that he didn't follow through with the order. He didn't think Daniel was serious. "You realize you are just a kid?" He could not imagine a kid so young could have that much money.

Daniel told him not to worry, just to send the equipment quickly. Daniel told Ron how we tried to speak to at least twenty other salespersons who simply dismissed us. He told Ron he felt he was very kind, even if he had just assumed we were kids having fun at his expense. For that kindness Daniel thanked him.

We have become good friends with Ron. In fact, we ordered all our farm equipment and parts exclusively from him, even all the farm equipment we purchased for use in other countries. After our order arrived, Daniel sent Ron ten thousand dollars to further show our gratitude for his acceptance.

That trip worked out well, but there were many other times we wanted to buy something and the salesperson wouldn't even talk to us.

Email to Washington:

The town received a very large shipment of farm equipment. Do you think they are going to grow more aliens? I saw a movie once where the aliens grew from seeds. Have your guys investigate the supplier. Who knows, he might be one of them. Have you made any progress with the President? We should have prepared for their receiving shipments of who knows what. From now on, I will have everything that goes in and out of that town inspected. We might even be able to plant some listening devices. To date we have been unable to restore our surveillance system in the town. We have tried aiming listening devices at them, but no electric signal penetrates their border. You have never been here to see this place. Actually, there is nothing to see. The town where they live is five miles from an invisible barrier. To prevent accidents, they have eliminated all roads approaching the border directly. They rerouted major highways so they do not cross their territory. Those bastards paid all the expenses of the highway changes. There is an out station where truckers stop, call in and wait to be met. Even if you walk through the woods, once you reach their border you just can't go on. It's the damnedest thing. Imagine what we could do with that?

We built a great school system. The buildings fully climate controlled. All the latest in technology. We had our own computer laboratories, creating our hardware as well as most of our software. The teachers are experts in their field such as math, literature, etc. and well trained and carefully monitored for effectiveness. A number of children from outside of our town attended our schools. All students were provided with a computer in class and another for their home.

There is a teacher for every five students for the first three years. Not the same teacher, five different teachers each day teaching for one hour. The subjects taught are reading, math (in every math curriculum we include the study of capitalism), writing and typing on a computer, art, and music. The teachers were well paid and carefully monitored. Students are frequently tested, not only to mark their progress or to see if the student needed help, but also to see if the teacher showed a pattern of ability or a pattern that needed correction.

In the fourth year and for the next three years there are ten kids per teacher. This has the same system of rotating teachers with the addition of two hours of vocational training. In the seventh year the students worked in groups of fifteen mainly using computers, of course there was a teacher in each group. Many of us lectured at the school in our special fields. Mitch teaches an advanced math class, Daniel teaches botany.

Three-year-olds and up were required to attend school. The day started with a good breakfast, all the kids together for a half hour. The seventh graders and up have the same pattern: two hours of academic classes, two hours of art, one hour of lunch. Oh, we served no meat, only vegetables, no sugar drinks, only juice or water. After lunch they had two hours of academic classes, then two hours of music and art. After music there was a half hour of snacks, usually fruits and nuts along with a drink of water or juice. Then two hours of vocational classes. In our vocational courses we taught automotive repair, computer repair, tool making, wood working, etc. Every child was required to take all the vocational courses. No homework was assigned. If a student wanted to do extra, they could. They have computers and could contact any expert in their field of interest, even outside our community. We paid very well for their services.

We had no sports as part of our schools. Sports is taught by professionals in clubs that operate evenings and on the weekends.

I should mention we separated the girls from the boys. This was done for a few reasons. One, the girls mature much earlier than the boys. Secondly, girls tend to yield to boys; they simply allow the boys to appear smarter or rather they act to less than their potential in front of boys. We have no real explanation for this, but Daniel thinks it may have something to do with a nesting instinct. Well, for whatever reason we found that after high school the girls were less likely to defer to the boys particularly because the separation gave them well developed independent skills and leadership rolls.

The school year was ten months long. We picked up any student who did not live in our town and drove them home. There were a number of students, that lived too far to be picked up each day, so we placed them within our families. Where possible, we gave them and their parents a house to live in. If a student or their parents did not measure up to our standards, they were asked to leave, but the student could keep the computer.

Another program was our agricultural requirement. We had farms on which all students worked. We had advanced laboratories to perfect seeds, fertilizers, etc. Equipment was made in our machine shops. What we couldn't produce we purchased. The students in our school worked on the farms, in the laboratories, in our shops, and of course, they got paid.

All students took electrical equipment repair, plumbing, carpentry, automotive repair, and many other great courses to serve them in life. These courses were geared to give us the ability to be less dependent on the outside. Oh! We had great cooking classes. In fact, we started our own culinary school, which produced great meals.

We had a good music program. Every kid played an instrument. There were always concerts to attend; the performances were great. We had an art institute, many of our children are quite talented. Our town had both an ice-skating rink and roller, bowling alleys, great restaurants, movie houses. You name it, we had it.

Children in the tenth grade who felt they were ready for college applied. Some chose vocational careers such as cooking or electrical equipment repair. They were all sent for degrees in their fields, and we paid for everything. Even the vocational students attended the best school for their choice of career.

During the summer every student traveled to a country that interested them. They attended language camps while living with natives of the country, always accompanied by staff members. If their parents wanted to go, we sent them. We paid all the costs, even the salaries of the parents. Our kids made many friends, and some eventually joined us.

Most students chose partners by the time they applied for college. Most were male and female. Some were same sex; a few didn't choose. Almost all experimented in different ways. Our children interacted beautifully with outsiders. Many fell in love and formed life partnerships with outsiders.

We keep full DNA profiles on each person. Our geneticists are trying to determine which genes give us our powers. We believe that all people should have their DNA tested, particularly with so many fertilizations of embryos from anonymous donors. It is quite possible in today's society to be going out with your brother or sister and not know it. We also use the DNA to insure as great a genetic diversity as possible for our community. We had a major project trying to link DNA to various illnesses. In some instances, we were successful.

Email to Washington:

They are expanding their group. They cleverly use their school system to attract young people. They lure in the parents with free tuition and in many cases free room and board. Admittedly their schools are far superior to most of the schools in the states, but you would hope that parents would think twice about sending their kids to alien schools. They hire teachers who are extremely well qualified. The best in their fields. But it doesn't end there; the teachers never leave. They become one of them. They marry into the cult. Those that are married move in with their entire families and never leave. We can tell by the courses that they will not need the rest of humanity soon. They teach every subject, even knitting, and hair cutting. They build their own machinery. They build their own computers and even cars. It is incredible how they are preparing to eliminate us. One more thing— there are an awful lot of Jews in that town. We should look into that. You know how those people are. Almost all the positive stories about them are written by Jews. And the movie of how lovable EL was, that was produced by that Stanley Stainer and with a name like that, he has to be Jewish.

Email from Washington:

I agree that they are using their school system to expand their presence. They have grown in numbers tremendously. The State Department reports that when they travel to other countries they are recruiting. After every stay in a country, they apply for several visas for students to attend their schools. We have been told that they always sponsor the most gifted, intelligent students. With all their attorneys, the State Department can find no grounds to deny the visas. By the way, there is some talk behind the scenes that these aliens are part of a Jewish plot. We have no proof, but where there is smoke there is fire. Try to find out how many of them are Jewish we may be able to use that statistic. Do you think Daniel and his family are Jewish? We will trace their ancestry. No wonder they are so weird with all that philanthropy bullshit. If we could prove they are aliens and Jewish we can kill two birds with one stone. You are absolutely right; all their good press is from Jewish sources. I'll see what we can come up with.

After receiving our degrees, we all had jobs in our fields. I taught math in our town college. Daniel taught agriculture. All of the original group taught and worked on our farms or in our shops. Daniel worked on the farm all the time. He loves to be around plants.

We own many companies around the world. The government actually didn't know exactly what we owned. They had some idea, but we set up and/or bought companies all over the world, very diverse companies, with no visible connection to us. These companies funneled capital to the accounts that we used for our various projects. As for the powers, we tried not to use them in public. Any glimpse of us being different was pursued as proof that we were aliens.

Every student is taught investing and capitalism. Daniel pointed out the education system in the United States does not teach capitalism, even though it is the main economic system used. Most Americans know very little about investing, and this puts them at a disadvantage. Much of their lives are determined by economics. As part of the course, we funded any worthwhile project that might succeed.

All students were required to participate in our capitalist ventures. They bought and sold stock as well as real estate. In the fourth grade they were taught to see the parameters of investing and learned to measure risk. They worked with real money and could see their successes and failures. Some of our students are quite wealthy in their own right, even a lot of the outsiders gained considerable wealth, which they took with them if they chose to leave.

We made money in many not so obvious ways. From our desalination plants all over the world, we extracted minerals, gold, silver, and many other usable materials. The students in our engineering classes got hands-on training in these plants. They designed ways of using even the "waste" which pollutes much of the waterways around the world. One of our major goals was to clean the earth's water. We constructed several extremely large ships that hopefully still go to areas of dense pollution, areas with floating debris. They scoop up the debris and the water. The water is run through our floating desalination plant and then returned to the ocean. The solid debris is recycled.

We have the alchemist's dream: we can make gold. In fact, we can make any element. We were able to break down atoms and reconstruct them in our own laboratories. We take various metals, and by forcing them into an environment where the structure of the atoms is affected, we reconstruct the loose material into whatever metal we want.

Only our inner group knows what we are working on. Our sensitive research was done in our own laboratories to make sure only we knew the process and could control the use and gain from the results, either by implementation or selling the results. Especially when the subject of our research can be abused by the government; we guarded our discoveries very well. When a topic was general and the results could not harm anyone, we sponsored the research outside our community and payed for all the equipment and salaries. We required our students be hired and take part in all such research.

With the gold and other valuable elements, we had unlimited wealth. No one, outside of our inner circle, knew that we could create whatever element we wanted. Because gold was used as currency, we deposited it in many countries all over the world. The deposits were used to fund our projects.

Strangely, some of our great discoveries were blocked by the government from coming to the general public. One example was a dietary supplement that unclogged arteries, no more stints would be needed. Most heart attacks would become a thing of the past. A person only had to take one pill a day, for a period of six months, and slowly all the plaque in their arteries dissolved. We found no side effects. The AMA lobbied the government to stop it from being approved, and it wasn't, but other countries did approve it. You can buy it inexpensively in Europe.

We are careful with our research and would never market a product we considered harmful. What is approved or not approved by the government has nothing to do with the usefulness or safety of the product. Certainly, approval has nothing to do with the good of the public. We believe so much in our research our whole town receives whatever breakthrough we come up with. We have been so successful very few people in our town have died since we became a family.

We are not sure if we have conquered death, but it looks like we have extended life. Daniel said, "Whether it is that we will live forever or not doesn't matter because life is lived one day at a time. We must always enjoy the 'NOW' because that is the smallest and largest measure of what we have."

—6—

ONE THING I'M PROUD OF is we can levitate and I'm the one who figured it out. It all started because the boys had flown with EL on their bicycles and I didn't. They would tease me all the time. They knew how badly I had wanted to fly with them. It looked so cool, and really I wished I had been older. I figured since I could scream like EL and get the same effect, move objects with my mind, why shouldn't I be able to fly?

We had large completely empty warehouses on our property. I chose the most isolated one. It was about two miles from the center of town. I could use it with a high degree of privacy. Every morning, after breakfast, I went there for two hours. I had gotten nowhere after three months of feeling rather foolish, with no clue as to how to achieve my goal. I tried everything I could think of. If anyone was watching, I'm sure they would have thought I was a little crazy. You can't imagine how frustrated I was and discouraged because I was sure it could be done. I just couldn't figure out how.

At first, I just tried concentrating on flying. I would repeat in my head fly, fly, fly, nothing at all happened. I tried leaping off boxes, nothing. I ran and leaped, nothing. One day I was totally discouraged sitting on the floor, completely relaxed and very tired, as I sat there with my eyes closed, I saw myself flying, feeling within me the pull of gravity. I pushed back. Really after four months of achieving nothing, I was exhausted and was playing around in my mind as I relaxed. Then I realized I had lifted off the floor. But at the same moment, I fell and hit the floor hard. It hurt, but I was so happy—I did it! The pain was proof of my success. But try as I might the rest of the morning it didn't happen again.

I returned the next day determined to replicate my progress. But nothing happened. The same on the third day. I was beginning to think I had hallucinated. I kept trying. Again tired and feeling a little discouraged, I sat on the floor to relax. In my mind I saw the guys flying, and I reached inside me to project me riding along side them. I was doing this for a short while when I realized I was off the ground. I was moving around the warehouse. I kept my concentration for a while but lost it and fell to the ground. Fortunately, I wasn't that high, it still hurt.

I knew I could fly, repeating my process over and over again till I controlled my ability to lift off the ground. I carefully learned how to back off slowly so I didn't crash. I was so happy, I knew I could do it, but I told no one. Every day I practiced. I walked in, closed the door, and lifted off the ground. I practiced for a whole month in order to dazzle the guys. I even brought my bicycle and laughed all the time I was flying. After perfecting my bike-flying technique, I invited the guys to come see what I found in our warehouse. I was showing off and getting even at the same time.

Daniel and the gang arrived and were walking around trying to locate my discovery. I gave them fifteen minutes to get discouraged. Then I walked in with my bicycle at my side. They all simultaneously asked, "What did you find?" Smiling from ear to ear, I sat on the bicycle and began peddling around them. They laughed and tried to figure out what it meant, then I rose off the ground. You should have seen their faces. It was probably the same expression the Feds had when the gang peddled over them.

Everyone was amazed and thrilled repeating "do it again, do it again." They had a million questions while they were tuning into what I was saying and feeling the method I used to achieve my goal. They were spared the agony and pain of failure, but that made my achievement seem so much more. They practiced what I told them. It didn't take long before they were lifting off the ground. A few times they fell, but that just added flavor to the effort. Laughing all the time we flew around the warehouse not realizing we had been missing in action for many hours. Our families, worried, called our cell phones. Daniel told Paige to come to the warehouse. All the others invited their spouses. My future husband, Vinny, was there, of course.

When the wives arrived, it was the same story. They were told I had made a great discovery (they gave me credit). While they were trying to guess, the eight of us held hands and lifted off the ground. We were children just flying around. The wives started laughing saying it wasn't fair they wanted to fly too. They actually learned much faster than the guys. It is silly, but we were there for five hours horsing around. We thought of the game played in the movie *Harry Potter*, the flying around chasing a ball on brooms. The next day early in the morning, we were back practicing. Paige actually brought us brooms. Two of the guys brought their bicycles. It was great fun.

We decided to teach everyone to "levitate;" that was Daniel's word. We made it clear it could only be done in the warehouse. We certainly didn't what the government to see us flying around town. As it turned out, it was a good thing we developed the power and even more important that we shared it.

Email to Washington:

They are up to something. Our satellite has captured that bitch Kate going into a secluded warehouse on the far end of the town every day for more than four months. She's there right after breakfast for hours. At first, I figured she was having an affair with someone, but no one joined her. Then recently her siblings and their wives have been joining her every day for hours. This has been going on now for three weeks. Some of them have brought bicycles with them. What it means? I don't know. They are plotting something. I wish we had ears inside the warehouse. In my opinion, since it is an initiative started by Kate it probably will be offensive and deadly. We will continue to watch and I'll forward any information we get.

At an accident, we learned something about Daniel that we didn't know. It scared us because it was like a super power. We had no idea Daniel had such abilities. Anyway, the accident: we were driving along a highway going home from a baseball game. While singing and laughing talking over the game we came upon an accident. Other cars had already stopped to help. There were four vehicles smashed and burning, a gasoline delivery truck and three cars. Flames were everywhere, a number of people could be seen in the wreckage. We left our car and ran toward the fire. That's when it happened. Daniel, Paige, Vinny, and I found this boy. He had been thrown from one of the cars and was lying on the side of the road cut up and bleeding, badly hurt, in fact he looked dead to me. His body was bruised and he had lost a lot of blood. Daniel said he felt the kid's spirit and proceeded to place his hands on the child's chest. The moment Daniel touched the child he responded and began breathing.

I thought, well, maybe he wasn't dead? Maybe Daniel didn't bring him back to life? I didn't know, I only know what I saw and felt. The moment Daniel touched the boy, I saw the wounds healing. I felt Daniel calling the child's spirit. I also sensed Daniel felt he had made a mistake and pulled his hands away. Daniel held the boy in his arms, and I could see Daniel was crying. Within a few minutes an ambulance arrived the medics took over the care of the child.

I watched closely. When Daniel placed his hands on Jesse's chest, the wounds were healing and I was shocked. We long suspected Daniel had the power to cure because of many other incidents and some of the methods we had learned to treat injuries, but we never thought that he could bring people back to life. Many times we saw him revive plants right before our eyes. But to bring a human being back to life is really a big deal and more than a little scary.

After giving statements to the police, we left the scene two hours later. The child made a full recovery. Stories about him appeared in the newspaper and on line. He was the "miracle child." The kid was the only survivor. His parents, who were not in the accident, were saying "Jesus had intervened."

Jesse's parents appeared on television telling the press how Jesus came to their son and brought him back to life. Jesus had "answered their prayers." Realize they didn't know he had been in an accident until the police contacted them two hours later. Positive prayers can help, but not in this case. There is no way they were praying for the boy at the time of the accident; it sounded good.

The doctors said the child had severe wounds any one of which should have killed him. What they could not explain was some of the wounds showed signs of healing. The boy, Jesse Chance, became the new darling of the news media. They ran stories about the "miracle child." His parents were on television giving thanks to the Lord for saving their son.

After Jesse recovered, he gave testimony in his temple. Thousands of people came. People wanted to touch the child "God had touched." People paid to come meet the boy God had saved. The media loved it. He was paraded from town to town. It was his turn to give interviews. I'm sure he had a media secretary to collect his fees. We hoped the money was invested wisely.

The night of the accident, we questioned Daniel. He spoke of feeling the need to heal this child and realized he had brought him back to life.

"It was a mistake to alter the course of reality." He shouldn't have interfered, but he was happy he did. Daniel feared someone might figure out he had brought Jesse Chance back to life. This would only add to our worries, giving our enemies another "oddity" to prove we were not human; no one ever did. They would see his power to bring back the dead more dramatically at a later date.

Daniel explained, "In a world where new world consciousness was a minority, we appear strange and threatening, a real danger to humanity. Look what they did to EL. It wasn't just because he was physically different. It was because EL was an advanced being, with advanced technology and his presence diminished the importance of mankind in the universe." Daniel says our group is an advanced form of humanity and must be very careful. We must not use our powers openly, to do so would only further the desire of the government to eliminate us.

Over the years, we followed Jesse Chance. He was quite smart but really not like us. He became a preacher with a great following. We became his number one target. Calling us "godless freaks." He inspired people to hate us. We learned he was working with the government and received funds to denounce us. Daniel said, "When a person gets too much praise their identity is diminished, praise destroys their moral being."

Daniel says "we should all love life. Love is respect for the power of good. We should help everyone we can. If our help is not wanted, that is okay. There are many other opportunities. When we help others, we learn and grow. The fastest way to learn a subject is to teach it. The teacher and the student both learn. Teaching is helping and helping is love in action."

Daniel says "we should always honor the wisdom and knowledge of the past and love our teachers. We should learn to enjoy what we have, not hope to enjoy what we don't have. If someone else has something interesting, enjoy them having it rather than wanting what they have. Wanting what others have eats away at who you are, you lose enjoyment of your own life."

We should always "set aside a part of our week to appreciate the universe and the life force we have. Take a moment to relax and give thanks for our lives, our families, and our friends." This idea we incorporated into our lives. We do no work from sundown Friday until sundown Saturday. We spend the time with friends and family celebrating the fact of our being.

Daniel says "a hurtful person, one that injures others, is not meant to be loved. But, should never be hated. Hatred destroys the person who hates. We should not hate those that mean us harm; we should just make sure they can't hurt us. To relive the pain of what was done in the past wastes precious moments of your current life. Going over what you think happened is not as important as the life in front of you. No one should ever throw away the NOW for the clouded memory of yesterday."

We were always working on protecting ourselves, particularly from the government. A good example of why were so paranoid occurred one day when we were flying back from one of our project sites. It was normal for us to inspect the work being done. We could make first-hand assessments of the progress and what might be needed. It was also an excuse to travel.

It was a four-hour flight on a commercial airline. We felt safe with 200 passengers and only twenty of us. We did not think the government would deliberately hurt so many people. Also, there had not been any physical attacks directed at us. The news media was always on our case, always finding a way to write a negative story. Extremists had marched against us, but we had never been physically attacked by the government directly, until now.

About two hours into the flight, most of the passages were either watching television or sleeping. Suddenly the plane lost power. We could feel the nose dip and all the passengers started screaming.

Daniel quickly asked us to tune in, (link up mentally). We were listening to the inner force of our linked minds. Daniel directed us to think of levitating, to see ourselves flying the plane. We knew how to levitate and jokingly flew around the warehouse playing games. We never actually thought of doing anything like this. We could feel the enormous energy generated by our combined thoughts. All twenty of us thought "flying," pushing against gravity. Daniel directed our energy to an image of the plane slowly coming down, the way we landed on our bikes. It was exhausting, we could feel the plane level off. We felt Daniel directing the plane toward the ground.

Through Daniel, we could see the ground approaching. The plane came down like a helicopter in an open field with no power nor energy except our linked thoughts controlling the plane. When the plane softly sat on the ground there was an outcry of tears and cheers. All on board were relieved the plane landed safely. Immediately the flight crew instructed everyone to leave the plane and gather in the field outside.

The crew and passengers said it was a miracle. Everyone hugged each other and were crying, including us. We felt such a relief, grateful we could help and of course that we survived. We were exhausted from the effort it took to levitate such a large object. We said nothing to the passengers about what we had done. We just joined in the celebration and waited for help. The flight attendants served a great meal and as many drinks as wanted. It took about an hour for help to arrive. The local people were wonderful, transporting us to the nearest hospital and then to an airport to continue our journey. Twelve hours later we arrived in California. The whole town came out to greet us.

In reviewing what had occurred, we found a major national newspaper had carried the story that Daniel and some of his followers had perished in a plane crash. The story was attributed to a government source. It had been distributed before the plane lost power. We later found through analysis, that a government satellite sent a signal to bring down the plane.

While now we were positive the government was trying to kill us, the government realized we had much more power than they imagined. It was clear the government wanted us dead and was willing to kill others to achieve that goal. We had to be very careful, after that we only flew in our own shielded planes.

Email from Washington:

The cabinet has accepted our evidence and now realizes we are dealing with aliens. It was a hard sell to the President, but finally he gave the military the OK to take them out. The plan is to go into effect tomorrow night. Daniel and his central team have purchased plane tickets on a commercial carrier for 8:00 p.m. tomorrow night to California. About two hours into the flight the military will send a signal from a satellite to shut off the plane's engines. We are very sure that falling from 50,000 feet will achieve all we hope for. They will be disintegrated in a pile of rubble. Be ready to move into the town and take the rest of those bastards into custody. Without their leaders, it should be easy. By the way I'm sorry, but that Kate is with them. I know how you wanted to get your hands on her, but don't worry, I'm sure there is lots of pastry in the town. Tomorrow we celebrate.

Email to Washington:

That is really good news. I will count every minute till it's done. All is ready here. I'll give the story to our friends in the press so all America will know they no longer have to worry about those aliens. It really sounds like a great plan. I didn't know that the military could do that, but it's good to know for future missions. Another great thing is that it can never be traced back to us, the plane had a "mechanical failure." That is all they will find. Yes indeed, we celebrate tomorrow.

Email to Washington:

What went wrong?

Email from Washington:

We don't know what went wrong. The signal was sent, the engines shut off, the plane went down, but it landed flat on the ground, no wheels, no crash. The plane just sat itself on the ground. It was described by some of the passenger as just floating to earth like a balloon. We have no explanation. One thing for sure is it has something to do with those aliens. One crackpot theory being offered by the military is that the kids levitated the plane to the ground. If that is the case, if they can do that, then there is no doubt they are not human. What is worse—it means they are extremely powerful and we must rethink our approach to eliminating them. By the way, how could you give the story to the press before you were sure it had succeeded? If anyone examines the time line we could be in serious trouble.

Sometimes I think of when we said goodbye to EL and we were taken into custody. We didn't want that to happen again. We did everything we could to protect ourselves. We were positive the government, if it could, would have killed each and every one of us. They would have eliminated "the threat." But, of course, they would first torture us to get our secrets. Our women would be abused as a clear demonstration of power. Throughout history this is how it always is. We were not going to allow it.

Daniel said, "When we say the government would kill us, we are referring to individuals, 'good people,' who work for the government and consider it their duty to protect what they believe in from threats (real or imagined). These 'good people' are the ones who sit around and plot to kill us. They give the orders that other 'good people' carry out. Just ordinary people doing 'their duty.' They are the protectors of freedom, 'just doing their jobs.'

"The role and job title of 'good people' dominates and dictates their behavior. The job overrides thoughts and beliefs. The role creates a morality of its own. If you can give them a good sounding description of their purpose, they become enthusiastic. Tell them it's for 'national security' or to remove 'weapons of mass destruction' and they are even willing to go to war. They never need proof. They just need a good slogan."

Daniel said, "You can see this behavior in the past. Look at what the Nazis did. A handful of men set in motion the murdering of millions of people because they decided Jews were not real Germans. There was no physical or visible difference. These few men just decided the Jews had to die. They thought nothing of having sex with the object of their hate. Many women were kept in camps for the pleasure of the staff while their husbands, children, and parents were killed because they were a 'filthy subhuman group.' The deaths were carried out by ordinary 'good people' just following orders, doing their jobs. They had positions that compartmentalized what was being done so they were not to blame. There was a 'good person' just gathering some Jews. There was another 'good person' who saw the gathering went according to schedule. There was the conductor of the train on which the Jews were packed like cattle, he only 'delivered the cargo.' There were the doctors who separated good workers for the factories, and good specimens for the laboratories so that 'human progress' could continue and they could do experiments with live human bodies. The remaining humans who were sick, or old, or just children, or women not worth having sex with, the doctors had them 'mercifully' killed. There was the scientist that made the gas so the extermination would be quick and 'humane.'

"We are the latest objects of hate from 'good, god-fearing people.' The person that pressed the button to send the signal to disable our plane was only 'doing his or her duty.' If you asked them why they did it, they would say, they were just 'following orders,' they were doing their job."

Back in California there was such anger and calls for retaliation. Daniel pointed out most of the anger was coming from the women with me as their leader. Daniel said, "it is a natural instinct for the women to react to protect the group. Even though we are peaceful in our intent." Daniel said, "Kate would be in the lead." I was more than a little pissed. Daniel took my hand and said in front of everyone, "Not now, Sis; no one was injured."

What we did was to close access to our town. The town was completely shielded and no outsider could come in without a careful inspection. What I wanted done was for Daniel to order our brokers around the world to start dumping securities and gold on the open market. That would be a good lesson for the government. But Daniel said a lot of innocent people would lose their savings, their jobs, then their homes. I realized he was right; we were not hurt. I still think it was a good idea.

We used every safeguard we could think of to protect ourselves, particularly when dealing with the outside. We often found goods cheaper to buy than produce; parts for equipment, frozen food, and other items. We only ordered from set vendors with a fixed protocol. An order was placed, the items were delivered, payment was immediate. Many times we had to pay top dollar on the black market, particularly after the government decided we were the enemy. You would be amazed at how willing almost everyone was to sell to us. Even individuals who openly called for our elimination. I mean money can buy anything. Unfortunately, as protective as we were, still we were hurt.

One August day, the town was so peaceful everyone doing their own thing. A large shipment of frozen food arrived. Our procedure was always the same. The truck was driven through very large detectors to check with scanners for any hidden devices. Then one of us would go out and drive the truck through our shield while the driver waited outside. This was a shipment from one of our regular suppliers and we knew the driver.

We always used the same procedure. We bought the load and the truck. We drove an empty truck similar to the one we drove in out to the driver.

We gave the driver the truck, paid him or her for the load and the truck and included a generous tip. This we found was the best way to handle deliveries. The money certainly encouraged many to deliver to us.

We had many precautions in place to check the shipment. The frozen food was unloaded and placed into one of our many refrigerated warehouses and could not be used until checked by our biologists. This batch passed inspection and was served as a side dish in our high school. A half hour after eating the corn, students and teachers got ill, vomiting and running a fever. None of the medication we normally used helped. All our doctors converged on the town. They reviewed the blood work and our laboratories examined the corn. At first, they found nothing.

We assumed it was an attack, but we soon received reports of the same illness globally. Many deaths were reported. Then one of our geneticists, while reviewing the corn's DNA, came upon an odd sequence and was able to connect the modification of the corn's DNA to the illness. A remedy was found and immediately reported to the CDC, the problem was the DNA modification of the corn. We also supplied the antidote.

The CDC was grateful and immediately distributed the antidote in the US and to all European countries, Australia, Japan, South Korea, China, and a few other Asian countries. But apparently, they did not deliver the antidote to any African countries. When we became aware of this, we contacted a pharmaceutical company in India we owned and gave them the antidote. We wired them fifty million dollars and asked them to supply the medication to Africa.

Email to Washington:
They are susceptible to poisoning. The recent corn DNA problem affected them too. We will search for ways of poisoning their town. See what you can do to help. I'm sure that there are some chemicals somewhere that we can use untraceable to us. You have all those scientists working for the government. I bet some of them would be very happy to get a grant to study the problem.

Email from Washington:

Already I have our scientists researching chemical agents to wipe them out. This could be a breakthrough. Unfortunately, someone intervened with the opportunity to wipe out a percentage of Africa's useless population. There are so many resources in Africa we can't get our hands on because of the silly people that live there. Maybe we can use whatever our scientists come up with to get rid of the aliens and the Africans?

The corn was recalled, without identifying the reason. From then on, we added DNA testing to everything we bought. You would think the CDC would have ordered DNA testing after what occurred? No, they did not. It is amazing how economic and political decisions get in the way of doing the right thing, even to the extent of putting the general public in danger.

Email from Washington:

I have arranged with some of our friends in Congress to have Daniel called in for a hearing. They will try to get that alien on record as an anti-American. When Daniel and his buddies leave the Hill, use that special group you have and let's see if we can inflict some damage. At the worse we can have our reporter friends show how hostile they are. Try to video whatever action you take and make it look as if they attacked us. Do whatever is necessary to make them look like aggressors. I have already notified our friends, and they are anxious for this to work. Our follow-up will be to declare them a terrorist group. Then we can seize their assets and make it a crime to trade with them. They still have to eat and with a little luck we can starve them to death. I know you want to get your hands on the women. Pull this off and you can have them all. We are still working on the poisoning angle.

The worst attack, at least the scariest one for me, occurred when we were leaving Washington, DC. Daniel was called to testify before Congress, an inquiry about our building subsidized self-sufficient homes for people. This was only one of many reasons why the government wanted to question Daniel. He didn't want to go, particularly after what happened the last time. As always, the questions were all over the place. It was evident the members of Congress were just demonstrating they were doing something to stop us. At least this hearing didn't end with them screaming at us.

When the hearing was over, we went to lunch, then drove to our plane. In our cars just leaving Washington, on our way to the airport, road work brought the traffic to a standstill. Slowly we inched our way forward. There was no rush our own plane would wait for us. As we came alongside the work crew, about one hundred workers in repair crew gear, a stop sign was held up, so we stopped. They opened fire with all kinds of weapons. They just kept firing. They had placed bombs under our cars which exploded lifting us up, but it did no damage.

It was scary, but with our shields there was nothing to worry about. When all the shooting and explosions stopped, most of the attackers were dead, killed by their own weapons. We waited for the police but instead another larger, heavily armed group arrived and continued the attack. It was crazy. Daniel decided we had to leave. It was obvious the police were involved. We did what we never before publicly did, we levitated the cars and moved away while the workers just kept firing at us.

We felt badly, but there was nothing we could do. As soon as we arrived at our plane, we took off. I alerted everyone to lock down wherever they were and return to our town. Those in the town were to stay put.

The news media had headlines the next day "Daniel's alien followers killed 860 road workers." An entire story describing the automatic weapons and our two hundred armed followers. Do you believe it? We attacked? What was worse, the public believed it. The media inspired protest marches; television programs were denouncing us.

Daniel said, "The government was defending humanity; we should try to understand their point of view. We are an advanced human model possessing something they will never have." I understood what he was saying, but I really didn't like it. I told him we should strike back. He just smiled at me and said, "Not now, Sis," unfortunately the attacks continued. They had visual proof we were aliens. They saw our cars lifting off the ground and flying away.

Email from Washington:

They can't be touched, but we got the public aware of just what a threat they are. I'm sorry you lost so many members of your team. The videos showed the workers being killed and we juxtaposed clips of the aliens in the middle of the death scene. You did well; I'm putting you in for a promotion. I do wish we can get our hands on that force field. Now we have confirmed on camera that they can fly. The media is having a field day. Great job.

Email to Washington:

Thanks for the promotion. The progress you've made with Congress is paying off. We really got the public going. I think we should plan more of the same, particularly, now that we have the public and press on our side. It was a shame that so many died. The good part is that they weren't our men. They were hired just for this job. They were a bunch of ex military out of work. I recruited them at the VA. We paid them well. So we really lost nothing. Too bad, but that's the way it goes. Those aliens seem physically untouchable with that force field and flying away like that. We will get them. I'm still waiting for the poison. Probably putting it into their water system would be most effective.

Email from Washington:

We have had a meeting with the military. They are now concerned that the aliens are becoming more powerful. They were very alarmed by the way they attacked those road workers on the highway. There was a long discussion about the force field and how it would be an asset if we had control of it. But they couldn't understand how a car just lifted up and flew to the airport. The car was left at the airport and there was nothing found in it to suggest how it flew. It was just an ordinary car. In fact, we had shots fired at it and the glass broke. There was nothing to explain the shield. The only difference is that the kids were the shield and they made the car fly. The meeting concluded with good news; the President has authorized the military to see what they can do to stop the aliens. AT LAST!

After the attack our entire group came to California. While we were gathering, we were attacked again, suddenly missiles disintegrated against our shields. It lasted about an hour. They just wanted us dead. This aggression was against our whole town, a town full of women and children. The next day, an analysis revealed it was carried out with radioactive devices. The radiation was everywhere outside our shields. The government told the news media we had attacked a neighboring military base. It made the front page of all the newspapers and there was a CNN special showing the destruction we had caused. Many people were joining in the chorus asking the government to get rid of us? The hate could be heard, seen, and felt, and it was so sad. We were gathering anyway, but this added to the task of trying to figure out what we should do.

Email to Washington:

How do you like the scene we arranged? That military base wasn't fully in use. We destroyed old barracks and put uniforms on a bunch of Mexicans we hired for the day. We didn't even have to pay them. The "aliens" killed them. We even got CNN to buy the story.

It is amazing how easily the government uses the media to manipulate the public. It is not always the media's fault. Daniel said, "The public is not aware enough of their own lives to be able to make intelligent decisions to help themselves. They can't see when they are being manipulated." There was a candidate for governor in the state of Wisconsin who ran on the promise when he was elected, he would dismantle the unions and their contracts. He won the election with many union members voting for him. When he started dismantling the unions and their contracts, the workers were angry and tried to have the governor recalled. It was too late, he actually carried out his promise. Most union power in Wisconsin has been weakened and will probably never recover.

The candidate said what he intended to do. The workers did not connect what the governor said to their own lives. This is a good example of the general public's failure to recognize what is in their own best interest. That is why it is so easy for the government to manipulate the news. The public blindly accepts what the media presents and never takes the time to ask whether the story is true and/or how does it affect their own lives?

The government through the control of the education systems makes sure that the general public do not really become educated. (Realize this never affects the wealthy. They can afford to send their children to the best schools). If new ideas arise to improve the system, the government finds groups to oppose the changes. If testing is a good measure of a student's development, then why not also use it to evaluate the teachers? That is how to create opposition, teachers' needs against the needs of the students.

Because of these and other shortcomings, the general public accepts what the media says and what politicians tell them. Daniel pointed out a good example: a very large part of the American population say they don't want the government to interfere with their lives. They see no reason to have to pay taxes for "those people. They say the government should get out of the medical insurance business, and social obligations. They argue this, even though most of them and/or members of their families are collecting social security, Medicare, Medicaid, veterans benefits, food stamps, Section 8 housing, or SSI. And still, they argue to eliminate government subsidies. If their goals were achieved, they would be hungry, evicted, with no health coverage. They just don't see it.

Daniel says "most people never see what is in their best interest." They adopt the teachings of whatever group, enjoying the status the group gives them. They only subscribe to the media that supports their views. Even though we had done nothing to harm anyone, the media said we had, so it was okay to attack us. Needless to say, we were disappointed by the government's attacks and the media's lies. I just wanted to hit back, but Daniel kept saying, "Not now, Sis."

What the attacks did was to hurt us emotionally. Intellectually we understood why we were being attacked, but emotionally it hurt. After all, we were Americans. We were born here and grew up here. So did our parents and many of our grandparents, even some of us could trace our families back to the American Revolution. My sister-in-law, Ebana, can trace her family back to 1820. The earliest member of her family she found was a slave on a plantation in North Carolina,

We are all Americans. Our whole aim had been to better the lives of as many people as we could. We paid our taxes and contributed to the development of better education in the world. We did nothing wrong. I guess you can tell by my rambling how hurt I was. We all felt betrayed by our government.

Email from Washington:

The military is frustrated by their inability to penetrate the shield. They have thrown everything they can think of at them with no results. The aliens are so arrogant they actually enter and leave their town even when it is being attacked. We are looking for some suggestion as to what we might do. You are the closest to them, so come up with a plan. The one thing the attacks have done was to wet the appetite of the military for their technology. We have many new friends among the top brass. The President now understands what we have been saying all along. The cabinet no longer laughs at me when I bring up the aliens. The CIA director has a "problem" with "our analysis." He says there is no evidence that the "kids" are aggressive. I can give him the long list of all the good people they have killed. Not aggressive my ass.

There were many reasons the government attacked us. One was our electricity generating fuel cells. This cheap electricity took a large financial burden off the backs of the middle class. We mass produced them and sold them inexpensively to whomever applied.

Daniel said, "People appreciate better what they pay for and abuse what they get free," that is why we charged. Every building we erected came with fuel cells. The cells generated all the energy needed and excess electricity was sold for a profit to the local utility. The cell ran on water. You just put in water and you got out energy and water, yes, it gave back the water.

We had installed them over eight years in five million homes. One day a company showed up claiming they owned the patent. We thought it was a lie. Research revealed they had indeed perfected a very similar device thirty years earlier. They secured a court order claiming we owed royalties for all the cells in use. So, we bought their patent for twenty billion dollars. Privately we asked why didn't they produce the fuel cell and market it themselves? To our surprise they said the government paid them not to produce it. Buying the patent enabled us to continue providing the cells. We accelerated our production of homes and built thousands of fuel cells. We had warehouses full of them. It's a good thing we did because later we needed them ourselves.

Daniel explained one way of controlling people was to keep them in debt. The monthly cost of electricity takes a large portion of a family's income. This limits their choices. The way the government controls young adults is through student loans, they are locked in the need to pay back the money. Not all students; the students from wealthy families don't have any debts. They are free, and their choices are unlimited.

About four years after we bought the patent, the government came out with a report stating that the fuel cells were giving off radiation and were dangerous. The news media and the politicians were all over it. They scared people. Even those who had the cells for many years believed the lies. Groups marched against us believing our fuel cells were part of our effort to eliminate the human race. Like, we aren't human? The government said the devices would explode. Even though there was no scientific evidence, the government brought scientists to testify how dangerous it was to be exposed to the radiation being given off by the cells. The cells that converted water to hydrogen and oxygen then used the hydrogen to generate the electricity, it was really sad.

Congress passed a bill outlawing the use of the fuel cells and all the cells were removed from the homes. The government provided no interest loans to replace the system. The loans could be paid back as part of the monthly electric bill. We could do nothing. I do want to point out the cells remained in use in all other countries around the world. In addition, all generators used to produce electricity in the US are powered by our cells.

The public believed the news media, which published the government lies. There were headlines, the aliens "endangered the safety" of American families. That the devices would lead to the destruction of mankind from radiation poison." It was sad the public accepted it.

Anyone interested could find books and articles about the fuel cell. There is no mention of radiation. In fact, many articles applauded the cells because it had no health side effects and was safe for the environment. On television, in the newspapers, and on the internet, the cells were said to be bad, everyone believed it. Many government leaders testified with great concern and earnestness, how the American way of life was threatened by our attempts to destroy humanity. And the public believed it.

Email from Washington:

Great job getting rid of those generators. It took us a while, but finally we have better control of the lower classes. Those generators account for a large percentage of the alien income which they will no longer receive. The media was easy. The hard part was to get enough scientists who needed money to testify how dangerous those cells were. It cost us millions. We literally are now funding about one thousand research programs that we have no idea what they are researching. We actually had to buy a building and construct a laboratory for this one group. But in the end, it's worth it. They have been cut down a notch. One good thing is that some of those scientists are working on trying to figure out the protective shield. Who knows? They may come up with something.

-7-

THIS MAY BE A GOOD TIME to explain us. Who are we? We are now a group of middle-aged "kids" who had the wonderful experience of knowing EL. When he left, we discovered he had given us something very special, the universe. We became a big family. All of us that were in the hospital together came out as one unit. One persona mentally and emotionally. After leaving the hospital we simply expanded our presence. Daniel became our leader.

Daniel is absolutely special. He is the gentlest person you could every meet. He is soft spoken and thinks every person is good. He never got over how the government treated EL. To this day, and with good reason, Daniel does not trust the government. He simply could not understand why any intelligent human being would want to hurt the first real contact with another species, particularly a lovable being like EL. It is obvious from EL's relationship with us he meant no harm. We definitely benefited from our contact with him. We realize we are different than most people on Earth. We have evolved to the point where we interact with nature in ways the rest of humanity can't even imagine.

Anyway, about us, we lived our lives like everyone else. We had a few advantages, we are extremely wealthy, we think very clearly, we can link up mentally, oh! we can fly, toss objects around with our minds, throw lightning bolts, and are not able to be touched. Other than that, we are perfectly normal. (smile)

We respect all life and work for the betterment of mankind. The only advantage we had, that was respected and admired by all human beings, was our wealth. We were, collectively, the richest group of people in the world. We actually had more money than 90 percent of all the countries on the planet.

Daniel is our leader. He doesn't give orders. In fact, he is very quiet. We can feel through him a harmony to our lives. His only title is Chief Botanist; he watches the crops and supervises the agriculture research laboratory. Daniel married Paige, they met in elementary school. She is the chairperson of the education committee. Her specialty was setting up schools around the world. Together they have six children all of whom are very intelligent. Their children also have our powers, my children do too. That is how we are certain we represent a genetic change even though we have not yet isolated the gene. When I say they have our powers, I mean they can learn them, not born able to fly for example.

Daniel and Paige lived in a modest home. He loves new inventions and employed them immediately even though some turn out to be duds. He tries his best to help everyone. He always speaks of love and our responsibilities to humanity. Daniel feels I have to be held in check to avoid outsiders getting hurt. He tells me to be gentle in my responses. When I say let's retaliate and attack, he says, "Not now, Sis." It's a little annoying.

My brother, Mitchell, married a girl named Ebana he met at college. Mitchell is chairperson of our mathematics department. He heads our math research center. Ebana is in charge of all our money, chief financial officer. She also teaches advanced accounting courses in our schools. They have five kids and also lived in a modest home. Their children have our powers. Mitch and Ebana had an apartment in New York City where Ebana grew up. They loved to attend Broadway shows and went frequently to the East Coast. Some of Ebana's family have joined us and are part of our group.

I'm Kathy, Daniel's sister. I am chief operating officer, coordinating our personnel and organizing any rescues that might be needed. I married Vinny. He is six years older than me, but we get along very well. Vinny is our chief investment officer. He coordinates with Ebana where we should invest and then monitors the investment. Daniel says I'm very aggressive and must work to not want to always get even. But it's just that I'm not as forgiving as Daniel. It always seemed to me, short of killing someone, some of those people who wanted to hurt us should have been taught a lesson.

Don't think I don't love everyone, I do; I just love jerks less. In my mind you're never going to be safe if you just take the nonsense and do nothing. I have eight kids and they all have my view—you must do whatever is necessary to survive. I've noticed particularly my five daughters are ready with a good argument to stop the stupidity of aggression. (I never tell them "not now kids.")

My mother, Mary married Kiel; they are happy together. She is a housewife who spends a lot of time dressing up and going out shopping. Kiel was an FBI agent who hunted EL, but he really is a nice guy. Because of his police background, Kiel was put in charge of our security. He is a good example of a thinking human being. He realized the injustice of persecuting EL and what they did to us, so he joined us. It helped that he fell in love with my mother. He is great to have around, especially for our kids to whom he is like a grandfather. Boy can he tell stories. Especially about how the government closed in on our family while we were hiding EL. There is the added bonus of my mother being extremely happy. Especially since my father and his wife live in our town, in fact, right next door to them.

Gary married a girl named Asha he met at MIT. She is originally from India. Gary is our chief electrical engineer, and Asha is our chief mechanical engineer. He was in the hospital with us. They have five kids. All his kids inherited the change.

Tom married Gary's sister, Terry. Tom is in charge of medical research and Terry is one of our leading pathologists. They, too, were in the hospital. They have eight kids with the genetic change.

Stan married Sharon, my sister. Stan is our chief civil engineer. He maintains our town. Sharon is in charge of logistics. She makes sure we have all the supplies and equipment we need to keep our town going. They have nine children with the change.

All the original group, from the hospital, and their spouses, make up the central committee, which makes all decisions for our group. Our town was one big family and accepted new members all the time. We had the largest concentration of intelligence on Earth.

Daniel is special and is the key to all of us. We derive our gifts from Daniel. Daniel noticed he could heal cuts just by touching them. He found when he touched a plant, it grew. If it was a flowering plant, it bloomed. He realized he could anticipate others' thoughts and actions. He could tune in to other people's minds and feelings. This was difficult for him at first, but he learned how to tune out negativity.

Email to Washington:

These aliens are really promiscuous. They reproduce like rabbits. This is more than just their women being oversexed, although I'm sure that has a lot to do with it. Do you believe each family has on average six kids? Some have ten and more. I wouldn't be surprised if all the kids have been fathered by Daniel. You know how those cults are, the guru gets first dibs. They see him as their spiritual leader and are reproducing a lot of hims. He probably goes to bed with his sisters in order to further the alien clan. You know, keep the blood pure like the pharaohs who married their sisters. There must be over six thousand kids in that town. I'm sure they are being trained in preparation for their attack on humanity. I'll keep you posted.

Daniel can repair anything. It is as if he has a blueprint in his head of everything created. He can look at an object, and in a few minutes, understands how it works.

Daniel realized when he held us in his hands, he could transfer his being. He said when he encountered us in the hospital, he was so happy. He visualized our inner forms and felt the necessity to hold us. He could see himself melding into our essence and an enormous necessity and desire to bring us into his sphere. In his hands we become special. He held each of us with our head between the palms of his hands and we, in that moment became one. He gave us what EL had given him. But not entirely, he can do things that absolutely amaze us. We know he has much more power than any of us; he just chooses not to use it.

Over the years our group has grown. People just fit in. We could feel their inner being and knew they were one of us. Very few members of our town have our powers. What makes us the same is we are all new-world people sharing the responsibility for humanity. This is the result of a world-wide cultural change, a change that is linking new-world people together. We with powers are the cultural change and a genetic change. My family was born with it. Others received it directly from Daniel. We had everything we need because of our enormous wealth; the government couldn't cut off our access to the finances. The money was well hidden all around the globe and it maintained us and funded our projects.

In many of our companies, people from outside of our community were in charge. They had no idea we owned the company. Daniel, in spite of the fact he didn't trust the government, was smart enough to put family members of congressmen in high positions in all our companies, some were in charge. Daniel said the greed of high salaries and the possibility of losing it if they connected the company to us kept our investment safe. If an outsider raised any questions, their senator fathers or congressman parent would step forward and point out how silly the idea was. They protected their self-interest and, in the process, protected us.

We had everything we needed in our town, shops, and great craftsman who made whatever we needed. Usually, it was quicker and easier to buy what we needed outside. We were self-contained with plenty of energy and water. The problem was we were cornered and were followed wherever we went. Even though we really can't be physically harmed, it was emotionally upsetting to always be under attack.

Everyone looked suspicious. We could leave our town whenever we wanted. We were well protected and can fly. We also have very effective offensive weapons. The problem was other people got hurt when they attacked us. The people being hurt were just workers, it wasn't their idea that we were the enemy. We didn't want others hurt, and we ruled out attacking them. (Well, I hadn't). It seemed to me we could give them a good lesson, which might make them stop.

Daniel believes we were a new form of humanity even before EL arrived. That is why it was so easy for us to accept and understand EL. We also evolved culturally, as have many others around the world. A cultural change that unites a large part of humanity.

Our universe is built on love, respect, acceptance of all, but more we embody within us the understanding of the power of the mind to achieve anything. Daniel says "the only true union mankind can achieve is through love. The love we share opens us to each other and the greater positive force of the universe."

We are different than most human beings. As a group we can concentrate in such an intense way as to make it possible to achieve anything we want. Even though we are physically the same as all other human beings, we are feared. Feared because we are a new genetic form of humanity. In time our kind would have come to dominate the whole planet. But not in a way that would have hurt the old genetic type. We had no reason to hurt anyone. All humanity is linked. If a section of humanity doesn't change to the new-world ideas, they subconsciously wait to die. They know they are no longer relevant to the species. Not changing culturally has the same effect as not changing genetically.

You can see dysfunctional behavior of those that have stopped developing. They fall into repetitive patterns to prove they are relevant. Look at groups that deny science. They come up with the strangest explanations of reality. Some oppose vaccines, even when their children get sick. They say things like "it is God's will." They denounce those who believe in science. It isn't enough for them to just believe in what they believe; they want to eliminate those who disagree. They hate "them," and they hate new ideas. They know what they profess is not really the answer they pretend it is.

Hate destroys such groups and destroys their kids. Their children grow up with name-calling and open discussions of hatred and killing. Hate destroys all relationships. Fear is what takes over. They live in a culture where everyone bullies everyone else. Because of the fear, they need to protect themselves, and they carry weapons to deal with "them."

It is very sad; groups that deny change know they are not superior. In fact, they know the other model is dominant. They just fool each other with a make-believe politeness. Every member of such a society is a victim. They all live in fear constantly trying to prove they are right and the outsiders are wrong. No one dares to contradict their teachings.

Their intelligent children leave and rid themselves of the negative feelings. Their new-world children have an inner love for humanity their elders can't accept. The parents hate those kids because they become "outsiders." There are many of these groups. They don't just hate change, they hate themselves. One interesting note, the children that move on are generally still loved by their mothers. Daniel said, "most victims of hate never really experience it. They feel what they have been taught and the lesson dictates their actions. They interpret every nuance as limitation on their development. Women often are able to break out of the limitations. Men are locked into a memory of a reality that may exist but certainly can be ignored if a proper goal is developed. The goal has to be formulated as something that is achievable in the majority culture. Once set in motion it just happens. The person who achieves their goal no longer fits in, for they can see it is the behavior within their community that keeps its youth from being able to enter the main culture."

We are fortunate to have come together and have Daniel to lead us. We are blessed by the power of love, which gives us access to the universe. What we can accomplish is unlimited. Our accumulation of wealth is a good example. We felt with all that money we wanted to do all we could to contribute to humanity and make the world a better place.

Our plan was to help our planet in every way possible. We identified various problems mankind was facing and set up committees to select the ten most urgent and then put together a plan to yield a solution. Once a plan was in place, we figured out the financing. Members of the central committee were put in charge of getting the job done.

The ten most urgent problems we came up with were:

1. Global warming
2. Oceans rising
3. Lack of rain in many areas
4. World hunger
5. Lack of educational opportunities
6. Lack of health care globally
7. Lack of housing
8. Lack of infrastructure in many third world countries
9. Enslavement of women
10. Lack of opportunity for older people to retire

Solving the rising oceans problem would actually solve the lack of rain, global warming, and world hunger. Our main project we pursued was to lower the level of the oceans and raise the water table of the aquifers around the world. These projects created more rain to help grow food, thus reducing world hunger, as a bonus, the rain lowered the temperature of the atmosphere.

To lower the sea level, we identified places around the world where the ground level was substantially below sea level. Working with the United Nations, we advanced our solutions. We fully funded the projects, paid all the expenses of research and planning. These were presented by the United Nations to the countries involved. The UN secured the cooperation and negotiated the details of how the projects were to proceed. They also settled who would be in charge of the sites and negotiated the wages for the local workers. When all was in place, we purchased the equipment and provided the funds needed.

The easiest project was in the Libyan Dessert: a place called the Quttara Depression in Egypt. The depression is fifty miles from the Mediterranean and about thirty miles west of Dabaa, Egypt. Two pipes thirty feet in diameter were laid side by side in a trench dug to the Mediterranean Sea. Many people were employed. The thick plastic pipes were encased in three feet of reinforced concrete so even if the pipes deteriorated the channel would remain open. The digging started at the depression and took one year to arrive at the shore. The idea was simple, because the land was so much below sea level, the water would just flow naturally to fill the depression. The best part was it worked.

Much of the water, at first, was absorbed into the ground. It took several months before the water was visible and started to form a lake. It was more than a year before anyone would say there was actually a lake. It only looked like mud for a long while. The lake produced clouds as the water evaporated and rain fell east of the lake. Whole towns developed near and around the lake. We paid for the building of the towns. We built desalination plants that purified the water, a hospital, schools. We built the infrastructure with sewers and sewer treatment and fresh water piping systems. The streets were laid out and housing was constructed with roads leading to other cities and the coast.

Even though, I said this was the easiest one, it took a number of years to get started. There was opposition from different groups. Plans had to be presented, and we paid off quite a number of politicians and clergy. We viewed the payments as the price of doing business. Don't think this was unique to Egypt. No, every work site required payments. Once the project was started, it was done rather quickly. Even fish came in with the water. Through our hidden charities we continue to fund all the schools and hospitals. Education and health care were two other priorities achieved by building schools and hospitals at each site.

Another project—the digging of a trench one hundred miles with two thirty-foot pipes to allow water to flow into the Dead Sea. Again, it was a great success. There was less opposition so it was accomplished rather quickly.

The biggest of our projects was in the Sahara Desert. It took ten years. The others only needed a trench and laying of pipes, but this one required the digging of an enormous hole two thousand feet deep and ten miles in diameter. While the pipes were laid, six hundred miles to the Mediterranean. The project was delayed by the discovery of cities no one knew existed. The sites were completely excavated before work continued. They dated back six thousand years. This created a whole new branch of study.

It took ten years, but once the gates were opened the water just flowed. The five-pipe system is incredible. It took four years for the water to become visible so much went into saturating the ground. New towns developed with industries and farms. The Sahara started turning green. Four years after the lake became visible it was discovered you could dig a well and find fresh water one mile from the lake. Apparently, the ground acted as a natural filter.

We did the same thing in central Australia with the same results. Also, a very long set of pipes were laid from the Arctic Cycle to Mongolia. This took a long time but was a great success. The ocean level of the world was lowered about four feet. The increase in evaporation lowered the earth's temperature. The water, of course, allowed millions of acres of new land to be farmed,

These projects were left in place and not destroyed by the governments because we took no credit. Publicly it appeared as if the UN had sponsored the plans with the help of local governments. We should have done the same with the fuel cells. Daniel said it wouldn't have mattered because the cells gave independence to the users. The lakes required government control.

We built desalination plants all over the globe run on our fuel cells and solar energy. They were left in place. Most of the world's electricity is generated with the fuel cells.

The hardest and saddest project sponsored was in the South Eastern Sahara Dessert. The systems were put in place and the pipes laid. But all was destroyed by fanatics, who, with images of divine intervention, brought an army of willing believers and destroyed the pipes. What would have helped millions was destroyed, leaving the people to die. In the Northern Sahara people were happier living longer with fresh water. It was beautiful to see the transformation. Where, thirty years ago, there were no people, now there were hundreds of thousands, where there had been no cities, now there were homes, schools, and hospitals. Where there had been no water, now there was an enormous lake. Healthy people living in beautiful cities. The cities were built with strict sanitation codes, sewage plants, underground water, and sewers, and street lights powered by solar energy.

Some problems developed. One of the biggest was the new areas attracted a large number of immigrants. The various countries reacted differently. Some simply shot the newcomers. Some put them in camps. The most amazing thing, however, was the UN actually came up with a plan, they issued world identification papers based on DNA and fingerprints linked to a worldwide data base.

You would be surprised how many people leave their own countries because of need. The need to eat or have a job, the need to take care of their families. You would be shocked, we were, by how many people arrived at their new home and then try to destroy it. They were not happy in their old lives and they tried to replicate that unhappiness in their new lives. This behavior was very difficult to understand. It was obviously linked to how they saw themselves, but it made no sense. Why some people left a place where they were persecuted and went to a new home and tried to replicate the persecution? We could not understand.

Because of this strange behavior, all immigrants were tested psychologically. They were also tested for skills and aptitude. If they did not have a skill needed, they were sent to school. They were asked not to have more than two children. They were taught about pregnancy and contraception. If they had children, the children had to be immunized. The children ages 4-16 were required to go to school, including the girls. If there was any objection or none compliance the person or persons were sent back to the nation they came from. Some groups refused to be tested, some refused to educate their girls, some said they had their own laws to follow. All such groups were sent back to the country of origin and people from such groups were carefully scrutinized before they gained entry into any other country.

Housing was provided, which they were expected to purchase. Once they started working, they were required to continue doing so until retirement, at which time they received social security and health care. If they committed a crime or if there was any objection or noncompliance they were sent back to their own country. All this was supervised by an international department under the United Nations. There was an incentive for the immigrants to assist in the maintenance of the system. The training in vocational, academic, social, and linguistic aspects of the environment helped them to integrate quickly to the new culture. The system worked fine and created an easy way to bring labor to areas where it was needed.

Another project was the central US aquifer. Eight pipelines were buried across Canada to bring water through a large number of desalination plants into the central United States where the water was distributed to the farmlands. This provided unlimited water for crops. The pipelines came from the Hudson Bay area. The water soaked into the ground and fed the central aquifer. Plans were put in place to divert floodwaters from the Mississippi, Missouri, and the Ohio rivers to four large man-made lakes that served as reservoirs. The land for the lakes was purchased at fair market value. This helped, not only flood control, but also irrigation.

On the West Coast of the United States, a series of desalination plant were built, about six hundred of them. This supplied fresh water to the region. Interestingly, even though there was a water shortage, there was a lot of opposition to the building of the plants. Anything from not near me, to they will make the West Coast shoreline ugly. Strange? The West Coast was becoming uninhabitable and an obvious solution was opposed. They were built anyway.

These were some of our accomplishments for which we did not get nor did we want credit, even though we planned and paid for it all. To us it was a great pleasure to have helped.

I do want to mention something we were very happy to have accomplished, Chernobyl. Our scientist found a way to neutralize radiation by changing the atomic structure of the material. We offered our services to Ukraine. It took only ten years and today all the radiated land has been returned to use. The future possibility of the reactor spilling more radiation was eliminated. It wasn't easy; the main reactors were accessed and we converted the radioactive elements into nonradioactive elements. This was the same process we used to make gold, obviously, we did not share the process. The problem was that we became visible. Our team directly ran the project, in charge of the entire operation, and they limited who could have access to the site.

To have done these things gave us a great satisfaction of purpose. We had contributed to the betterment of mankind and that we feel is the reason for our existence.

Email from Washington:

The aliens have a team of engineers working at the reactor site in Chernobyl, in Ukraine. Our ambassador in Kiev has reported that they have special permission from the Ukraine government to access the reactor. We have been unable to ascertain exactly what they are doing. The government of Ukraine is telling this cock and bull story that they are "cleaning up the radiation." They are probably harvesting the radioactive material to make a bomb. I have alerted Home Land Security to inspect everything they carry away from the site. I'll keep you posted.

Most people can't begin to imagine how terrible it is to be constantly stalked. I guess celebrities do, but they are not physically attacked with the intent of causing harm. We know what it is like. Even though we can't be harmed, it is a terrible feeling to always expect the worst from humanity.

Cornered here in our town, protected, with plenty of provisions, we can hold out probably forever. Even though we can go anywhere we want, it's not the same as being free. The real problem is the government wants our technology and are very willing to kill us to get it. Slowly the government put together a list of all our powers. They became obsessed with finding a way to acquire our technology and eliminate us. There was no subtlety about it either. They openly inspired groups to attack us, they joined in, and the attacks were endless.

Email from Washington:

Be ready to move on them on the West Coast. We don't want his sister, Kate, coming to the rescue. Tomorrow we plan to throw a net over Daniel and drag him and his shield into captivity. We have high hopes of success. The net will hold him and his shield while we drag him to a secure location where we can figure out how to disable the shield. Then we can kill him. Without Daniel the group will probably sue for peace. The only other obstacle might be his sister. But, if we're successful, we'll get her too. I know, when we have her, she is yours. The plan looks really good. Everything is in place, and we will have their technology, finally. Then the possibilities are endless.

(If we had read this email on time, Daniel would have avoided the whole incident. This is a good example of the difference between gathering data and being able to use it. We had so much data we just didn't get to it).

Email to Washington:

Great news let's hope it works. I'll throw everything I can at their town to keep them occupied while you "net" their leader. If it works, she's mine. I'm looking forward to getting my hands on that Kate. She has had eight kids, so I know what she likes to do best. Even after eight kids she is so damned sexy. With me she'll experience a real man, not the nerd she married. Back to business, I have about twenty thousand assets at my disposal; we will move on your signal. The plan sounds like it will work. We might still have the problem of getting through his shield. But I guess, we can starve him to death. Then there will be no shield. I'm sure you are right, without him the rest of them will probably surrender.

Fearing we were getting stronger, a group of government agents again tried to arrest Daniel. Daniel was leaving a meeting. He had interviewed on a national network explaining the safety, and energy-friendly nature of our fuel cells. It was an exceptional appearance. Daniel very rarely addressed the media. As he and two others walked toward his car a group of police officers grabbed him, or tried to. More officers tried to grab him but couldn't. They fired weapons at him. Daniel got into the car and was about to drive away when a net closed around the car and lifted it off the ground. A large steel container truck was ready. They were lowering the car into it when slowly the car and the crane lifted off the ground. It looked strange (they showed it on TV). The crane flying along dangling the car. Over a park the crane came gently to the ground, slowly tipped over and placed the car on the ground. Daniel then just drove away. He was sorry he had to openly use his powers while TV cameras were on him, but he was not going to be arrested and experimented on, not if he could help it.

Back in California we experienced a surge in attacks against us with the same results. They were hurt, we were laughing at their stupidity. Our concern was for Daniel whom we could feel was being attacked. We were quickly relieved when Daniel called to say he was on his way home.

Email to Washington:

He got away. I saw it on TV and am amazed at the power that kid has. To see that crane flying along and realizing he was controlling the whole thing with his mind. That is just incredible. If we can get that power, who knows what we could do? Good try. Our team did all it could with no results. We lost two thousand personnel and one thousand pieces of equipment. I'll send a full report next week after we complete an inventory. I will also send an accounting report in order to receive the funds for whatever needs replacement. I will have to recruit more bodies to be trained and ready. It's a good thing there are so many unemployed veterans.

Email from Washington:

It seemed like a good idea. The plan was approved at the very top. What we did not count on was how powerful he is. He may not be an alien to some, but they certainly have to admit he has superhuman abilities. It is obvious we have to find a way to neutralize that force field. The military is working on an idea. We will soon see if it works. The best part of the whole episode is the press coverage. The country now has clear proof he is not human. And even if they believe he is human, they can see he is to be feared with all that power. The pictures of him in a car flying with a crane attached is priceless. All our talking would never have achieved the proof that he is an alien seen in those videos. The best part is all the world could finally see it. As to the losses on your end, don't sweat it; it was worth it. Send your report so I can put in for the funds to replace the equipment; after this we will probably get anything we want.

The news media kept showing over and over again the crane closing the net on the car and then lifting it up. The narrative was that the government was trying to arrest the alien but couldn't. Then they showed the crane lifting off the ground and flying away. The media went on and on about how "America was endangered by these aliens. They must be stopped." They quoted anonymous high government officials as saying the military is working on other plans.

Because of these absurd attacks, I ordered the shields to be expanded another five miles out from the center of town. Our accounting department provided checks to the owners of the land and homes that were displaced by my actions. Daniel was a little annoyed, but he trusted my judgment and I had Kiel's support. We made sure all people living inside our new perimeter were escorted out. We supplied them with transport for them and their goods, and, in fact, paid them to leave. They were very willing to accept a million dollars for every member of their household. We paid them double the value of their homes and land. I viewed the taking of the land as a way of saying to the government "we can retaliate too."

Email to Washington:

Those arrogant aliens expanded their town another five miles. We are being told that the people living in the expanded territory are being evicted forcefully. There are reports of torture and the killing of some of the residents. We can actually see some homes being bulldozed. The residents are streaming out of the capture territory we will set up camp for them until they get settled.

Email from Washington:

Get the media on this. It would help if we had a few bodies to prove they are killing the residents. That shouldn't be hard to arrange. You have my go-ahead on that. We have so much support that we can get away with whatever the hell we want.

The news media screamed we were "taking over California." We had tortured and killed the owners of the property caught in our expansion. They had victims describing how we came and beat them. Two women said that they had been raped. They also showed the bodies of young Mexicans and their kids. Witnesses said we shot the family after violating the woman and the kids. The headlines "Aliens taking over the West Coast."

The only way we could explain these reports was that they were being staged by the government. A good example was the refugee camps with the tents set up by the Red Cross. There were at least 200 families claiming they had been displaced, forced out of their homes. Believe me, we made sure that every person that we displaced, including each child in the family, received one million dollars to move. With that much money why would they choose to sleep in tents? It made no sense unless the government and the press were fooling the public.

Email from Washington:

Really nice job, the country is in a frenzy to get rid of them.

The witnesses were incredible and the bodies. Where did you ever get the bodies? It was obvious they had been tortured. How many were there in total? Every news program had a different number. And those refugee tents. With the Red Cross feeding them, that was a stroke of genius. Did we have to pay all those people? Well, even if we did it was well worth the results. I liked that one person who described how, holding her baby in her arms, she went to take some of her family photos, she was pushed to the ground and kicked several times. Great touch really convincing. Great, great!

Email to Washington:
_____

You like that? The witnesses were easy, they needed the money. The bodies were three families of migrant workers, twenty-four of them. No one will even miss them. Actually, California is better off, twenty-four fewer wetbacks. We didn't torture the kids. The boys we just killed and made them appear like they had been tortured. We beat the shit out of the men to make it look authentic. We made them watch as we took possession of their women. But best of all we had great fun with the women. There were some real lookers among them. They put up a great fight, which made it more exciting. We really had a great time with their little girls, we figured that would really enrage the press against those aliens, as it did. We got the results we wanted and had fun in the process.

Sure enough, the government sent the Army to attack us. Most of our people were unaware of the attacks. The military couldn't get past our shields ten miles from the nearest house fifteen miles from the center of town. You would think they would have stopped their offensive when they hit our barrier? No, they opened fire with guns, tanks, bombs. Why? What large equipment they sent, like tanks or bombs disintegrated. The small arms fire just bounced back killing a lot of the soldiers. The news media said we attacked the police and killed a number of innocent civilians, that is why the Army was sent in. "The Military is defending America... containing the aliens so they won't further expand and take over the entire state of California."

The media was all over the battlefield showing the dead. It was terrible the lies they told. But, that's the media, our defenders of truth. We were helpless to convey our position to the general public. Even if we found a way, we would not be believed. The media usurps the "truth," and with earnest vocabulary, and the skill of the actors called "anchors," they feed the lies to the general public.

Email to Washington:

That didn't go well, but we achieved a media scoop. It was amazing. Sure, we lost a lot of men, but it was something else to see—the way the tanks disintegrated when they hit the perimeter of their territory. Even large artillery shells simply vanished as they hit the boarder. And the bullets that were fired from small arms just bounced back and wounded the shooter. We ordered them to keep shooting so we could have bodies to show the media. Boy, if we had that technology, we could tell the Russians and the Chinese to go to hell.

By the way, I'm not too old; I did two of those tamales and loved every minute.

—8—

WE WERE AT A LOSS as to what options we had. Daniel called us together to come up with a plan. I was so happy because finally we were going to do something. After a two-day discussion we figured we only had three options available to us:

1. we could stay the way we were,
2. we could take over the earth,
3. we could try to contact EL,
4. we could use some of our weapons and scare the hell out of the government, (number four never really came up, but I thought it would have been a great idea even tried to bring it up, but Daniel just stared at me and said his usual "Not now, Sis.")

We were sad because we were only trying to help humanity, unfortunately, everything we did was viewed as a threat.

We knew we couldn't stay the way we were. It was annoying to be constantly attacked and see all those people die. We didn't want to take over the earth. Believe me we were quite capable of doing so with our very effective offensive weapons. We decided our only real hope for normalcy, and setting ourselves free of these attacks, was to try to contact EL. We were sure he would have a solution. Our engineers talked over the problem. We had good transmitters to send out a signal but, a big but:

1. we didn't know EL's language.
2. we didn't know in what direction we should aim the transmissions,
3. we had no idea how far away EL might be.
4. we did not know if he would come (would he realize we were calling for help?)

Question number two, which way to aim the transmitters, was figured out quickly when Daniel, Mitch, and I remembered EL showed us where he came from in the universe. One night in Daniel's room, EL had levitated objects in the air to represent the galaxies and pointed out where his star was. It was a story we repeated many times because we constantly relived EL's visit. We immediately pulled up star maps on our computers and searched until we all agreed on the proper map and location.

Tom asked if we still had the old walkie-talkie EL used to contact his people? Fortunately, we did, we had retrieved it from the forest, surprised it was still there. Apparently, the government, because it was such low tech, didn't connect it to EL. Our engineers modified it and attached it to our transmitter, which we had used to send signals to outer space, part of an effort to contact other beings. We didn't know his language, but luckily, he left his calling card behind, recorded on the walkie-talkie, the message to call his people. So, question number one and two were answered.

We started transmitting the message in hopes EL would receive it, and realize we were calling for help. Unfortunately, a great number of years passed with no response. The years went by quickly, but we had hope. Daniel thought EL would come, but there is no way to say how far away he was, nor how long it would take for the message to reach him. Daniel said EL would come and maybe scare the government or do something to help us. Daniel was sure EL would have the answer.

Email from Washington:
They are up to something. Our satellites have picked up very powerful transmissions of radio waves aimed toward outer

space. We have been unable to decode the message. We can tell it is very short but haven't got a clue as to what it says. We are trying to determine what they are transmitting and we have trained satellites to monitor that direction of outer space. See if you can determine anything from where you are. They may be calling their mother ship. Like in The Fourth of July with Will Smith. Whatever they are up to, we are ready. Stay alert and report back as soon as you have something.

We tried to consider what EL might do in our situation. We realized his choices would be limited. We were sure he wouldn't want to hurt anyone. The only thing we could think of was he might come and take us to another planet. This idea was only discussed by the inner group and not shared with the whole community. Daniel felt the more general and abstract possibilities gave the most hope to the community.

Email from Washington:
_____
We have hired over five hundred experienced code breakers to decipher whatever the hell they are transmitting and to whom. These guys are very expensive. You would not believe the salaries they get. So far the only thing they have told us is that the message is very short and keeps repeating. The pattern is the same. Our scientist say that it is a narrow very powerful and focused band transmission to a specific sector of the galaxy. For sure they are contacting their mother ship. We must stay alert.

The powers we have are seen as a danger to humanity because of the government creating lies about us. We had never attacked anyone. In fact, if anyone took the time to look at what we had contributed, we would not have been treated the way we were.

Daniel says the genetic change was here before EL came; it has nothing to do with EL. Whenever change occurs, there is always opposition. We were able to communicate with EL because of a change we already possessed. We were already the prototype of the new humanity before EL arrived. Out of love he gave us the ability to defend ourselves.

Because we share thoughts and feelings, we mentally mature faster and work though problems with less emotions. We have a clearer understanding of our motives and the meaning of our words. To say we are very close is an understatement—we share every free moment with each other.

In addition to the genetic change there was a major change in human culture, a new consciousness developed linking many people around the world. The young today embrace the concept of a positive force which they feel within themselves. Because of modern communications the concept is being shared and spread quickly. In this changed world, individuals are responsible for their own behavior; they embody their own morality. All new-world people are linked through the doctrine of love, which brings responsibility for humanity to the individual. Daniel says you can see the change in the literature, *The Hobbit*, *The Lord of the Rings*, *Start Wars*, *Harry Potter*, *The Hunger Games*, *The Twilight* series. All are about an individual reaching into their inner self and feeling the force. They live their responsibility to humanity by doing whatever they have to do to protect what and whom they love.

The emergence of the concept of the individual carries with it the responsibility of the individual to all mankind. This new-world word, individual, is the carrier of modern social consciousness. In order for anyone to be an individual, there must be respect of all other individuals. Each individual must accept all other human beings as individuals and respect the differences.

In the past cultural change was very slow. Today change it is very fast. The young adapt to the changes quickly because it is the world they know and experience. The young have no reference to any other way. The older generation cling to old world views and are reluctant to change.

A good example of the conflict between generations is the idea of hatred. Hatred of a person, a group, a race, a sexual orientation, or a religion is seen by the young as a denial of individuality. The young believe in freedom for every individual, all individuals should have the freedom of choice. Whether it is for abortion, marring whom they want, or the right to die, every individual has the right to choose. That is the nature of freedom of the individual. The young accept that "all men are created equal."

A major part of new world consciousness is the moral constant which compliments the awareness of individuality. That moral reality makes each individual responsible for their choices. There is no more the devil made me do it. The new world youth reject religious claims to exclusivity of knowledge. The youth reject institutions that exclude individuals and/or groups. Having a different belief does not negate their humanity.

Even though new-world consciousness is spiritually based, there is no intervening God. In fact, there is no God. There is a spiritual connection with all creation as a member of the universe. We are on our own in the universe.

Mankind's new model of the universe has no outside intervening being. It does not reject the presence of a force shared by the positive energy of the universe. It rejects a supreme being, and shifts all the explanation to the science of life, and responsibility to the individual. New-world people watch as the old ideas devour each other in a race to be the true faith defending God against the "godless ideology." Their theology is so weak they have to go out and kill people to defend their god.

Believing the universe is governed by a positive force manifested in love, a love we show by appreciation and service to humanity, is not good enough for "god-fearing people." They don't love, they only fear, which breeds hatred.

By helping others, we embrace within us the joy of love. It is the acceptance of the positive force in the universe manifested as love. Mankind is freed of the fear of god and becomes the embodiment of the meaning of god, the embodiment of the universe.

Daniel says "the new-world change forces governments to serve the people." Government agencies must work to meet the needs of the general population. Governments must work to better the conditions of the society by providing safety, education, health care, roads, protecting the water and food supply and protecting business so all citizens have access to the possibility of choices in their life. The government must protect the individual from aggressive behavior which is defined as that which causes pain or harm to another individual or group. If a government fails to protect all people, the new-world youth will take to the streets protesting the violation of the rights of others. They are marching to defend the rights of individuals, that is their responsibility.

The question was asked why are so many people against individual freedom of choice? Against the government protecting individuals and families with programs that provide assistance? Why are there so many people who would deny others health coverage? The answer is most people are not in contact with their inner self. They pay lip service to a god in whom they really don't believe. If they did, they wouldn't hate other human beings, nor would they get angry because another person receives help. They have erased the memory of the help they received. They deny the right of the individual to choose and the responsibility we have to each other because they can't feel the love generated in a universe of caring.

"The concept of the individual grows in an environment where positive behavior is measured in terms tolerance of others, acceptance of change, and service to humanity."

As new-world people become more numerous, they expect governments to be responsive to the individual, to protect the individual. Governments in new-world models are established around the idea of tolerance and freedom for every individual. Old-world fundamentalists feel they are under attack. Their view of reality excludes individuality. Anyone who supports freedom for gays, blacks, women, etc, are people to be eliminated because "those people" really do not understand "God's word." These hate groups will be short lived. Hatred makes them turn on each other.

The responsibilities of the individual to the rest of the human family will make more demands on governments. These demands will continue until the whole human family has access to health care, education, housing, food, and predictable laws that give everyone equal access to opportunities.

One of the most interesting things Daniel has ever said is "cultures that suppress the female of their group are throwing away half their brain power." A culture that does not respect women will never have a Madame Curie. I asked why so many cultures make women second-class citizens? Why is it those cultures can't see the effect of female suppression? Daniel said "all human change and evolution comes through the female. Over the centuries advanced cultures were overrun by more primitive ones. In most cases the advanced males were killed and the women were captured, raped, and enslaved. The women had the evolved gene and/or the advanced cultural knowledge which they naturally passed on to their children. These changes were mainly passed female to female. Males who were not fighters were eliminated. An intelligent but not physically inspiring male would die young. Few males would survive to carry the change. But all the girls who survived carried the evolved gene and memory of the cultural advancement."

Advanced gene and cultural transmission has accelerated in our present world. In current new-world culture, there is a partnership of the sexes, the union of intelligent males with intelligent females. New-world people value education allowing the intelligent male to survive and become attractive to intelligent females. Daniel says our change has appeared globally. A major change linking a very large portion of the younger generation in every country to one another. They do not have our powers. But they share our view of humanity and the responsibility we owe to mankind. They reach for explanation of the universe through education, and they reject an intervening god, believing in the power of the positive force in the universe manifested by universal love.

We have something more than just the change. Our powers are obviously linked to our direct contact to EL. Daniel said we had to wait. EL would answer our call and will clarify how we received our powers. We continued to transmit our signal, a little worried since new-world people have been killed and it had been many years since we called for help. We had no way of knowing if our transmission was even received. But Daniel said EL will come.

People with our values started popping up all over the planet, not a lot but a good number. They would become good scholars and on their own developed projects to help their communities. It was hard to accept that a society would attack and kill people who were working to help others. But for no apparent reason they simultaneously came under attack in many countries. Even though they were helping others, they were attacked and killed. We could feel the pain of their deaths.

We have survived because of our shields and our wealth. Wealthy people are usually not bothered, the law protects those that can afford to use the system. This is true in every country. The government, with the help of the media, had built up a case against us. They created reasons why we should be treated as the enemy of the people. When we helped Egypt with a water system, the news media said we were helping terrorists. You should have seen the demonstrations against us. We were called anti-Semites in the same papers that claimed we were a Jewish plot to take over the planet.

Email to Washington:

I went to them as you suggested and offered to stop the attacks in exchange for their shield technology. I explained that the shield would protect the United States from being attacked, appealing to their patriotism. They are always claiming to be good Americans. I was truly amazed at their town. It looks like main street USA, but it is extremely clean; the atmosphere seems to be air-conditioned. Everyone was very polite and listened to what I had to say, except that bitch Kate. She just stared at me the whole time. I must say that, if he wasn't an alien, I could really like Daniel. He is just a nice person. Nothing like his sister. I'm waiting for their response. In the meantime, we are keeping up the attacks.

Email from Washington:

Good, just try to keep up a dialogue. The military is working on an idea to get rid of their shield. Our state department has

*convinced all the governments, that understand they are an
alien threat, to reach out and eliminate anyone that seems to
be patterning themselves after Daniel's group. We explained
that their behavior was the result of their minds being altered
by the aliens. That explained why they were so sacrificial in
the pursuit of helping others. We were able to show that the
outreach was really a recruiting method. That they are building up their numbers preparing for the attack. There is no
real loss in eliminating the whole bunch of bleeding-heart liberals spreading their doctrine of equality. Imagine wasting
one's life helping poor people? The poor can't even play golf.*

Daniel said "over the centuries other evolved individuals have emerged; they were usually killed. Some developed followers before their death. But the disciples where unable to experience the consciousness of the master. They could love the word of the master. But could not understand, nor feel, how love and unity with the universe is reachable within one's self. They could not experience how love was a gateway to feeling the universe. What the followers did was to create rituals and processes. They figured with rit-uals, they might come to understand the message of the teacher. The mes-sage was corrupted by their limited understanding of the concept. They simply could not internalize their teacher's message.

"The leaders developed patterns to allow others to achieve what they thought their master had meant. They figured if you did ten of one act and five of another, truth would be revealed. They would then be able to feel the 'word.' Or if they dressed a certain way or ate certain foods, they would arrive at the understanding of the truth.

"The followers never understood that the coming of a 'teacher' has nothing to do with the teacher. It has all to do with how each individual fulfills their own search to be a teacher. Focusing on the teacher is mean-ingless. The individual must focus on their obligation to humanity, on the service they can render onto others, on the love they give their neighbors each day. In order to be a teacher, you must become a perfect student to the voice of all mankind. Almost all of the examples of the teacher are lost in rituals and correctness of behavior created to distract the student from their inner self. That is not to say that these groups did not serve a purpose in the development of civilizations."

Daniel explained these groups have helped to raise the overall consciousness of mankind. In their teaching, they organized human behavior and planted the concept of morality, this raised mankind's consciousness.

Daniel says change comes not just from genetics but also from changes in consciousness within a culture. When a society has a word for an idea, the word plants the thought. The society moves slowly toward the understanding of the word. For example, the concept of the "individual" only recently came into human thought, because of its newness there are many people that use the word but do not realize it applies to everyone; at the same time there is a growing number of individuals that live out the responsibility of the idea to its fullest.

Daniel says new-world consciousness sees clearly the responsibility of each of us to be our brother's keeper. We are all individuals, even those with whom we disagree. In today's new world, there is an increasingly large group who understand. They find their purpose in working toward the freeing of all individuals from the hatred of others.

Daniel said, "EL gave us a push to our own inner selves. This enabled us to tap into the positive force, a force we already possessed." EL gave us much more, he gave us the love of learning and the ability to concentrate, which allow us to absorb and enjoy the flow of ideas, and even better, we can share our thoughts. These gifts have allowed us to protect ourselves. We are safe because of our ability to examine a situation and come up with solutions.

Daniel said, "it is important to accept death. We are born, grow old, our body breaks down, and we die. That is it, nothing more or nothing less. What actually matters is how we live our lives, and the service we render to humanity."

Daniel had a very important question to answer. He realized he could bring a dead person back to life; the question was should he? When it came to the elderly, he decided death was a reward, it stopped their decline and ended or prevented much pain associated with the deterioration of the body in old age. He accepted everyone will die.

The death of a young person is a case for "intervention." They have much to offer and should be given every opportunity to contribute.

Because we have eliminated many major diseases most of our people will live longer. If a person desires death, that should be their choice. Ultimately, we choose our own destiny, and death is part of our destiny. Daniel was asked what if a person was not elderly, should they be allowed to take their own life?

He said, "Everything possible should be done to discourage any person who wanted to commit suicide. Our social workers, psychologist, psychiatrists, and the family should all reach out. We should intervene because life is so special; all of us are linked to each other and responsible for each other. To have a person want to leave life requires a good reason. But truly the ultimate choice would have to be theirs."

To me anyone who was not suffering, who wanted to die was making a strange choice. There is so much to learn in life, so much to do, and so many people that need our help. It seems like a waste to not want to be alive to contribute to the betterment of humanity.

Our group has an inner peace that gives us a positive view of everything. On the few occasions when we have felt anxious, we do deep-breathing exercises to bring our minds back into balance with our bodies. But we have many activities that we refer to as relaxing events.

One of our favorites is baseball. We love the game; it is a mental game, a pitcher against a batter. Our children bring the game to a new dimension. My son Ted is a pitcher and he is really good. He throws the ball with force then with his mind he controls the motion of the ball. Some fans thought that wasn't fair. Then they realized the other kids could anticipate the pitch by tuning in. Ted learned to throw without sending the thought, the batter had to learn to redirect the ball with their mind. The games are such fun. My daughter, Carol, is one of the best players. She bats about 280 with twenty home runs in one year. Remember, we live in California and play all year round. We sometimes play outsiders and our kids are careful not to alter the game with their minds. They do well without their powers. Yes, they have lost to outsiders.

EMAIL TO WASHINGTON:

These aliens have corrupted the sacred American game of baseball. Their kids have been observed controlling the ball with their minds. The pitchers curve the ball drastically and can even make it stop at the plate. The batters bring the ball where they want to. They have ruined the game. Even a fly ball they can mentally force to come to their gloves. This is probably a training exercise for their kids to teach them how to direct objects against others. This is part of the attack training they are working on. It is terrible that the great American institution of baseball is being used in such a disgusting way. We see them practicing almost every day. By the way, how are the decoders doing with deciphering their transmissions?

We have taken the kids to Coopers Town, New York to the Baseball Hall of Fame. The children love the trips there. They, of course, know the history and statistics of the game. Every group we have brought there have asked the same question, "Why isn't Pete Rose in the hall?" when they are told he was banned because he bet on games, the kids always quote Daniel "human mistakes don't negate great contributions." (Daniel originally said this about Nikola Tesla who was criticized as a noted adulterer.)

We all enjoy games. We have five thousand families with an average of six kids in each family. Large families are no problem, because of the high level of communication skills, and the children quickly mature. Our children are aware of themselves at an early age. They are aware of when they are learning. They read and absorb what they read and know what they understand and what confusion might be found.

At an early age our children ask questions to clarify their understanding. In effect they are constantly testing themselves. They interact with their peers to clarify ideas, and are easy to work with. Of course, children have limitations. They can easily see their intellectual immaturity when they interact with older kids. The awareness, helps them to accept their role in life and they look forward to the various developmental changes.

Our children have a right of passage—when they reach the age of thirteen, we have a party for the "adult." The candidate comes before the entire community and must thank his/or her parents for the gift of life. They read either an original composition or their favorite author, then we party. Oh, yes, we sing happy birthday.

We celebrate Thanksgiving, Christmas, Chanukah, Diwaly, New Years, Martin Luther King's birthday, Lincoln's birthday, Washington's birthday, Easter, Passover, May Day, the Fourth of July, Labor Day, and our absolute favorite, Halloween. In addition to the right of passage, girls all have a sweet sixteen party. One additional holiday that is very special is EL day, the day he left us. So you can see, we really enjoy celebrating.

Socially our children interact with each other and adults with respect and caring. They try to see how they can help each other. Whether it is teaching a younger person to read or to throw a baseball, our children know they learn more about a subject when they are teaching it.

They know about EL, and that we are waiting for him to respond to our call. It's like "EL call home" is our big joke. It is interesting even though we are all smart and share everything, a hierarchy has developed. It's not openly discussed, but Daniel is our leader. You can see the reverence everyone has for him. He is always being quoted. Me and the original few who saw EL are looked up to by the other families. Because of our unique experience with EL, my family is considered the first family of our town.

Daniel tries hard to think everything through, consulting with the inner group often. We have meetings with all the families in town. Also because of our ability to share thoughts, there are no hidden motives and the words spoken are clearly understood. Questions are genuinely questions looking for answers, there are no egos involved. No one asks questions to show how smart they are.

Our favorite holiday, as I have mentioned, is Halloween. Everyone knows the story of how we walked around town with EL. The kids all want to be him. We relive the moment we shared with him laughing and enjoying ourselves. We have the ritual of watching Stanley Stainer's movie on Halloween, it helps us experience the moments in time we shared with EL.

We have fun, even though, we mainly stay in our town; games, movies, concerts, and gardening. We love to read and read everything we can find. Spending a lot of time educating our children is a priority. The entire town takes part in their education. We don't correct our children's speech patterns; they will learn the correct way by listening to others. We don't correct their posture, or the way they laugh, or talk, or most often, the way they eat. All children do what they see the adults do, not what the adults say. The children correct themselves through imitation during socialization.

We enjoy our children and marvel at their awareness. We praise the smallest accomplishment with phrases like that's "great" or "well done." We never criticize our children or speak of them with negative ideas: like calling them "little devils" or "sneaky." Children become what you tell them they are.

Another pastime is satellite TV; we see all the movies. We love movies. Not all, but good dramas where a puzzle is put together to discover a truth. We absolutely love good science fiction (I wonder why?) We like comedies but only those that don't put down or make fun of other people. We do not watch movies where there is death or wars. We understand death and find no reason to feel its pain in a movie. We do not understand why death, even a stranger's death, is so easily accepted by outsiders. Any death, even in a movie is painful.

One of our charities involves orphanages. We funded hundreds of them all around the world. All orphans were tested and if found suitable they were brought back to our school in California. If they didn't work out, we returned them to the orphanage. We continued to support them and their education. The ones who stayed in our town were enfolded into our group. Many have married our children. In this way we gathered the smartest beings humanity had produced from all over the world. This also gives us a very diverse gene pool to insure a healthy variety of children.

We love to tell jokes, even Daniel. One day when he was speaking at a meeting, he said his wife, Paige, was really glad when he melded mentally with EL he didn't end up looking like him. Boy! did we laugh. Another time he said it is a good thing the basket on his bike was strong or he might have dropped EL. Once he was asked what was it like to fly on a bicycle? Daniel answered it was great; he didn't have to worry about getting a flat tire.

All our girls love shopping (we think it might be genetic) and of course the boys like to tag along. It is easy for a group to take a plane and go to LA, Seattle, New York City, even Paris or London. They just blend in, no one really knows most of the families in our town. They can recognize me and Daniel but very few others. Also, we have noticed that our black, brown, and Asian members are never mistaken for one of us. So, if we mix the groups, even if by chance someone might think that it's us, when they see the "minority," they dismiss the thought. So we always mix the groups when they go out.

Our children can buy whatever they like. We give them cash so they are not followed electronically. Interestingly they usually don't go crazy spending; they enjoy the trip. They talk about it for days. In many of the cities we have property, they can stay overnight if they want. The students attending universities in a visited city have a great time playing host.

Another way we relax is to take our children on trips. We go all over the world. Often we go to Disney World. We just drive out of our town. The government can't stop us our shields are always in place, in fact, we have perfected our minds to such an extent the we are our shields. At first the shields were generated by electrical devices, now our minds generate our protection. We still use electric shields for large areas like our town. In our cars or planes our presence makes an electric shield unnecessary.

Once arriving at an outing, the youngsters have a wonderful time. It is interesting when they make friends with an outsider. Some of those friends eventually joined us.

But a couple of times our trips turned into terrible experiences.

—9—

Email from Washington:

We have put into motion a good plan to eliminate the force field. The military is very optimistic. They intend to capture a bunch of them, not Daniel or Kate. We figure our targets won't be able to defend themselves with the same bag of tricks as those two. This will take place sometime in the next few weeks. We have to wait until they are in a position to be taken. The military has a secure location. They will use electricity or something. I'm not exactly sure what they will use or how it's supposed to work. I was briefed, but you know how scientists talk. We will see if it works. If it does, we have them.

One of those trips, a day at the zoo, ten girls and two teachers were on an outing to see primates. This was a third-grade class, eight-year-olds. They went by bus, an hour's journey from our town. Everyone had their iPads, and on the way, they reviewed the animals they expected to see. The trip had been pre-arranged with the director of the zoo. We had sent many classes to his facility, and he provided experts in the field to assist our children. We, of course, paid very well for this service, and always gave very large donations.

When the class arrived, the director's secretary was waiting and escorted the group. They were introduced to their guide. He was a young man in his twenties with a PhD in animal behavior. The girls and the teachers were delighted not just with his knowledge, but also because of how handsome he was. At each exhibit they were greeted by an expert on that particular species who lectured and interacted with the girls.

The trip was going well, as the children were about to enter, what was billed as a special exhibit, they were asked to check all electronic equipment to prevent the devices from interfering with the study of the brain waves of primates they were about to see. The study would "eventually help scientists to develop a complete map of the brains of all mammals."

Once inside they saw two apes attached to electrical equipment. They did not notice the doors were made of very heavy metal and were sealed behind them. In the main room there were two "scientists" behind a glass window in a separate room. While they were waiting for the lecture, they could feel the whole laboratory was in motion; they thought this was part of the experience, part of the tour.

A video was played demonstrating different brain probing techniques. They saw the use of PET scans, X-rays, etc. This went on for about an hour, the entire time they could feel the room was moving. Then it stopped. The scientists excused themselves and suggested everyone should eat their lunch. So the kids opened their backpacks and just started joking around discussing the film while eating.

Unbeknownst to the girls, outside there was a division of military personnel. The building had been transported to an electric generating plant on an Army base. The military was interested in destroying the protective shields. If it meant killing the girls, so be it; they didn't care. They were sure high-voltage electric current would destroy the shield, then they could start their experiments. If it worked, they would eventually be able create a device to attack our town.

The teachers and students suspected nothing. They were busy eating. The truck was a sealed chamber of thick metal to prevent electronic and telepathic communications reaching the outside world.

The military had everything ready. As soon as the truck arrived, they hooked it up to the electric generator. The entire building was charged with a high dose of electricity. The military could observe the effects through cameras inside the room. The primates in their cages were electrocuted and died immediately. The teachers realized they were in trouble. They told the students to tune in to each other so they could communicate to the outside world. They quickly knew they couldn't. The teachers asked them to analyze their situation and find a solution.

Two of the girls, Sarah and Karla began playing with the electricity. Sarah quickly figure out how to bring the electricity into her shield and then mold it into a form. Karla was playing with the form she made by copying Sarah. All the girls tuned in and began to mold the electricity. Outside the military observers could see the electricity had no effect, so they increased the voltage substantially. The girls were in no danger. They were being attacked and knew it. The increased voltage gave them more electrical energy to play with. The teachers told everyone to collect all the electricity into their shields. They didn't have a solution, but it seemed like a good way of controlling the situation. The military increased the voltage again. As the girls were absorbing the current, Karla just for fun made a ball of some of the electricity and hurled it, like a lightning bolt, at the heavy metal doors. As the ball hit the doors, they blew open and were partially melted. They just flew of their hinges and the outside world appeared.

Once the doors were open the girls walked out. What they were greeted by was thousands of soldiers with weapons. The military opened fire. Sarah who was visibly annoyed hurled a bolt of electricity at the soldiers, electrocuting them immediately. All the girls began to throw lightning bolts at those shooting at them. The soldiers ran for cover, but the girls destroyed and or melted whatever object the soldiers hid behind, trucks, buildings, cars, etc.

Once outside the teachers were in contact with us. I ordered a convoy of buses from the local area to their location. A group of us ran to our planes and flew down.

Meanwhile the teachers told the girls to continue to absorb the static electricity around them and use it to keep the soldiers away from the group. The girls were told to line up in pairs of two one teacher in front one behind. They started marching toward the gate. The teacher in front began to sing so they all joined in. They were singing "God Bless America." The teacher in the rear was communicating with our convoy.

At some point the marchers passed a building with an American flag, one of the girls ran and took it and raised it at the head of the group. Can you picture it? Ten eight-year-old girls marching singing "God Bless America" with the American flag at the head of their procession, while a very large military unit was shooting at them.

The girls marched toward the road. They knew the buses were coming. The military kept firing at them. Every time the girls got near a building soldiers hiding behind the structures would attack them. The girls hurled fire balls at every building, which burst into flames.

One girl must have hit an ammunition storage area because the explosion was terrible, smoke and dust flew in the air. At the gate, the girls marching in perfect formation, the American flag in front, singing on their way out to the road and felt relieved.

Once on the highway they stopped, sat at a bus stop, and started eating their lunch and snacks. The teachers kept guard. For safety they blew up every building they could see. If anyone approached, they were hit by electricity.

PICTURE IT, TWO TWENTY YEAR OLDS AND TEN EIGHT YEAR OLDS HOLDING OFF THE US ARMY WHILE SINGING GOD BLESS AMERICA AND WAVING AN AMER-ICAN FLAG.

They did not have to wait long. Within a half hour our buses arrived. Just before Sarah got onto the bus, she hollered to all "watch this." She turned in the direction of the main building off in the distance and hurled a bolt of lightning. The building went up in flames.

On the bus they all hugged, and Sarah calmed down. The bus drove to an airport to meet our planes. When we were back in our town, we gathered to hear the story. We were pleased they were safe. But, to say the least, we were very annoyed the government would try to kill our kids in order to get to us.

Daniel said "that will teach them not to attack our children." We didn't want to deliberately hurt anyone, that being said, he pointed out we were not going to sit and let the government try to hurt us. Daniel then turned to me and said, "Well, Sis, I bet you wish you were there?" I smiled.

We were very interested in the way Sarah had figured out how to gather the electricity and, of course, how Karla used it as an offensive weapon. Within a few hours we all knew how to remove electricity from the air and throw it. Someone said jokingly we should just carry a small generator in our backpacks on our next trip. Another said we were "walking Tesla coils." That really made our hair stand up, (smile).

The next day we waited to see what the media would say. The only story connected to the event was one about an earthquake at an Army base where several buildings had been destroyed and two thousand people died.

We decide that future trips would be taken with bigger groups and we would pack a bigger lunch. Daniel, smiled, saying, "Maybe we should teach the children new songs."

Email from Washington:

What went wrong? The reports I am receiving don't begin to make any sense. The girls did what? It reads like a kid's comic book. The whole military fort destroyed by twelve kids? There has to be an explanation more acceptable that I can take to the President. Were you there? what the hell happened? I avoided talking to anyone because I don't know what to tell them. I asked the military for a complete report. The only thing they said was they sustained heavy casualties. The military brass are just not talking. Your report reads like science fiction. What the hell really happened?

Email to Washington:

Yes, I was there. It actually seemed like the military had a good plan and was carrying it out well. They transported a small group of girls to the army fort. The girls were in a truck rigged to look like a zoo experiment. They arrived and were immediately hooked up to a massive electric generator. The truck was charged with electricity within two minutes after arriving. Enough electricity to kill the two apes in the truck. The military felt the electricity would break their shield. Once they were dead, we would have the bodies needed to test their DNA even better we would have a way of destroying their shield. All went well for about two minutes. We could see on our monitors that the electricity was having no effect on them. They were actually playing with the high voltage current as if it were a toy. Then all hell broke loose. The doors of the truck, reinforced steel doors mind you, were blown off their hinges and the ten kids and two teachers came marching out throwing fire balls at everyone. The military opened fire at them to which they responded with more lightning bolts that burned everyone and everything they hit. Believe me they were unstoppable.

Email to Washington continued

They had somehow gathered the electricity and were throwing it at everyone and everything. I hid. If I hadn't, I, too, would have been electrocuted. They threw the electric balls at every building, when the balls hit, the building went up in flames. They had the nerve to march in order with an American flag in front of them while singing "God Bless America." It was terrible. Really bad. A few years ago, I noted that I felt they were training the whole town to attack us. You can see even their children, at such a young age are trained militarily. When they started attacking our troops, they were in perfect military formation marching in pairs of two. Each side of the line responsible for the targets on their side. They weren't even sweating or crying like little girls should. They just kept attacking us for no reason while singing that silly song.

Email to Washington continued:

Everywhere there were bodies. Some looked cooked, some you could see on their faces that they had been electrocuted. Every vehicle was destroyed. Every standing building was destroyed. The electric generator was destroyed. They even destroyed the front gate. The estimated damage to the post is about 4 billion dollars. All the "girls" were just marching out to the road and singing. Who do they think they are to do that to a United States military post? Who do they think they are to kill our service personnel and destroy our property like that? If there is still anyone there in Washington that still thinks they are not aggressive shove this report up their asses. That is what happened. It's hard to believe, but that's what happened. This is another demonstration of how powerful they are. This, however, scared the hell out of me. Maybe I'm too old for this stuff?

Email from Washington:

I can't believe it. We have put out a cover story that there was an earthquake that destroyed the post. It is incredible, but 90 percent of the buildings are completely demolished. The loss of personnel was in the thousands. You are absolutely right they don't give a damn about any of us. Who do they think they are to do something so destructive to our country? You were right all along. Their children have received military training. That whole town is probably just one whole standing army ready to attack us. I agree with you, maybe the two of us are too old. The more we deal with them the more I realize it seems to be a losing battle. They are getting stronger every day. I am proud we have been able to keep the issue front and center. If we had not realized from the beginning what they really are, they would have hidden in some corner and then destroyed us from within without a fight. Old or not we can't quit now. We must protect the United States of America to our last breath.

A year after the zoo attack, we were on an outing to a beach we often visited near our town just twenty miles away. Unfortunately, we had another surprise. The beach was fun for the kids. On this trip we had taken about two hundred kids and fifty adults. They had their food, built sand castles, played volleyball and other games. Our kids loved the beach. Fish swam up to them and they enjoyed playing with the fish.

There were people from outside our town enjoying the beach with us. Most of their kids were friendly and there was nice interaction. Many joined in our games and shared our food and drinks.

There were about one hundred kids in the water, not all ours, they were swimming and clowning around, when a large number of motor boats appeared about one hundred yards from shore displaying American flags. They were aimed directly at our kids and were coming fast. We alerted the kids to the situation. They didn't panic, they held hands and placed outsiders behind them.

Our children understand the nature of our shield and how to effectively use it. As the boats came closer, we could hear the yells of hatred. The screams of "kill them, kill them all." It was terrible our children had to experience such hatred, worse was what happened to the boats. When they reached our children, the boats smashed to pieces. The collision with the shield completely destroyed them. The debris and bodies were everywhere,

We all ran to help. Our kids stood up on the water and first rescued the outsider children who were crying and scared. Then they grabbed as many of the injured boatsman as they could. The boaters were stunned by the impact. Many were injured. Some were unconscious. The ones that were aware were visibly shocked to see the kids walking on the water and pulling them to safety.

All of it was captured on video. It was a good thing we had our own copy, because the boaters claimed we had attacked them. Even though we had rescued every boater, their hatred was so great they were not just ungrateful, they were vulgar. They cursed us and spat at our children. They kept saying "they were defending America." They were "doing what the government was too scared to do." They at least "tried to kill the aliens." One side note, the parents of the kids we protected were very thankful.

It was difficult for our kids to understand the why of it. Back home we had a meeting and our social workers sat with the kids and their parents. Daniel told them he was proud of how they had protected the outsiders and helped the injured. He said, "It is very sad to come face to face with evil, we must all pray that these evil individuals will come to understand how they are destroying themselves with their own hatred."

The media, of course, went crazy with the story. They had eye witnesses testifying we had attacked the boaters and severely hurt many of them. The media had video of the event which they showed over and over again leaving out the part where the boaters tried to run over the kids. They only showed our kids walking on water. They even left out the rescue. They showed our kids dragging the boaters on shore and said the kids had beat them up. The videos were further proof that we were aliens. Plainly our kids could be seen walking on water. That was the story.

We received an invitation by one of the major networks to come and explain what the video showed. I accepted the invite. I brought a copy of our video showing the entire event as it unfolded. Their producer looked at it, but it was never aired. When they finally asked me about our walking on water, I pointed out it had been done before. I asked the reporters if they thought that the originator of walking on water was an alien? To that they asked, "Do you people think you are gods?" It did little good to confront the media; they ignored everything I said. I just felt good that I did. (Frankly, I felt like smacking the reporter when he made the "gods" remark.)

Email to Washington:

Did you see the complete tape I sent you of the boating incident? I was there. I just couldn't believe it. They pulled a Jesus on us. If you look closely you can see the kids held hands and created a protective barrier in a straight line. That is what the boats crashed into. I am always amazed at their powers. With their military training, those kids didn't think twice, when they saw the boats, they linked up. There wasn't even a signal sent, no one called out the boats were coming. One of them must have seen it and immediately mentally alerted the entire group. They are amazing to see. Even scarier is they stood up on the water and picked up the boaters carrying them to shore. Why do that? I would have let them drown if I were attacked. If we could only get our hands on them, not just the powers. Did you see some of the attractive women they have in their community?

Email from Washington:
_____

The video was very interesting. I like the edited version you gave the press. It clearly shows the freaks walking on water. Oh! I love the part where it appears that the kids are beating up and dragging the boaters. As you said if you look closely at what they are doing you realize they are trying to resuscitate the boaters. I have no answer as to why they would bother to help someone who attacked them. They probably thought it would gain sympathy with the press.

    On a more important note; Yes, it would be nice to get our hands on some of those women. Do you realize none of them are overweight? We should ask them what's their diet and publish a book. We can call it "The Alien Diet." Was that Kate in the yellow bikini? It doesn't matter who she is, she looks good.

Email from Washington:
_____

We have approval for a new project. Starting next week, we and our allies will quietly round up and eliminate all people who fall within the parameters of goody-goodies. We will eliminate bleeding-heart intellectuals who espouse the liberal point of view. We have also included people who run agencies and help the poor. All these categories we have identified as people who might be recruited by the aliens. This action will dry up their supply of new recruits. See if you can identify any in your area. I have asked all our agency personnel to find them and put them out of their misery. Don't worry about warrants or law enforcement repercussions. We have permission from the highest authority.

One of our major concerns was the safely of people who shared our values but did not have our powers. Our engineers tried to find a way of protecting them without endangering our technology. They could not come up with an answer. We decided to pick up anyone we felt shared our vision of humanity. Some were safe because they were not noticed but many others were in great danger. It was terrible the way intelligent people working for the betterment of mankind were disappearing.

We notified all who we felt were in danger, if they were willing, we would bring them into our town to safety. If they wished to come, they would be instructed what to do and where to gather. We planned to beam a force field around them, land, and take them away. It was up to them if they wanted to join us.

I led one of the rescue missions to Western Africa. I selected two pilots, two electrical equipment specialists, a doctor, and a nurse. Our plane was completely shielded with stealth technology. We flew at eighty thousand feet, much higher than normal flights. I also took along an offensive laser just in case (smile). Daniel says I shouldn't take a weapon because I might use it. I told him if I did use it, he can rest assured, I would have had a very good reason to do so.

As we approached, we transmitted our arrival and where we would come down, beaming a force field around the area. As they gathered, they were attacked by their government forces. Our shields protected them.

They boarded, and we quickly took off while the soldiers looked on with amazement.

On board there was such warmth and love that passed among us. It was a small group of ten women and five children. They wanted to stay in their own country to help their native culture, but they had already lost all of the adult males and were aware they probably would not survive much longer. The women had been beaten and sexually assaulted.

The rescues took about a month, we brought about six thousand families to our town.

Email from Washington:

We were right to kill those liberal bastards. We estimate we have eliminated about fifty thousand around the globe. There was some collateral damage but war is war. We have proof most of them were assisting the aliens. As we were attacking, the California mafia reached out and rescued quite a lot of them. We estimate that their numbers now living in their town have increased by about two thousand, but it could have been worse, they could have had another fifty thousand. This was a good operation. How did you do in your section of the country. You should have received the reports from your staff. I'm curious, send me the figures.

Email to Washington:

I and my team were very successful. We positively eliminated eighteen hundred liberal bastards in five states, mainly on the West Coast. I took it as a chance to even some scores, that was the best part. Some of us did enjoy the fruits of our labor, not all liberals are ugly. My staff has yet to compile the data. I will forward all when it's ready. We have observed planes landing frequently in their town but have no real count of how many people they smuggled in. If we could get our hands on them, we could charge them with smuggling illegal

*aliens into the country. (SMILE)! You are right, they would
have had fifty thousand more soldiers to attack us. This was
a good operation. We should have done it years ago. I never
realized I could enjoy a liberal.*

I often think of the hospital. Daniel in a coma being fed intravenously, everyone was concerned. When he joined us, he said his mind was reviewing the course of human possibilities, an enormous flow of data. It took him time to figure out what it was. He refined his ability to separate and review the information. To the outside world he appeared catatonic. No one could see what was going on in his mind. Daniel said the greatest element of his awareness was awareness of himself. He understood he was part of the universe and everything that exists was part of him. If he looked at anything with love, it would become part of his being. He would receive love back as acceptance and sharing. Even inanimate objects he could feel and the object became one with universe.

When Daniel reviewed human cultures. He realized he had come before, not him exactly, but similar advanced individuals with meaningful changes that briefly affected the human experience. Daniel understood he was the latest evolved being in the development of mankind. At first he thought that he was alone, but he quickly realized his family had also been born with the change. He received and refined his ability to concentrate on any subject until he totally understood it. It would reveal its inner meaning and essence and became part of Daniel's being.

Daniel said "everyone could achieve this experience if they concentrate and stay aware of what they actually know and what they do not know. Anyone who wholeheartedly loves the object of their thoughts would become the thought." Daniel felt the pain of continuous change. It was not only that Daniel learned to see clearly, he learned to see what he could not see. Alternate explanations of reality came to him and he felt the burden of choice and the joy of possibilities.

Daniel played out in his mind how each variation gave a different outcome, like a chess player planning his moves. He journeyed through what is and what might be, he became responsible for tomorrow. He realized that even though we think we understand something, we only understand it in the context of our limitations. Daniel says "we see only the limits of our vocabulary." We can only see and understand the words we have already identified. We cannot see new ideas until we carefully absorb them and develop a vocabulary for the ideas and use the new words until the words melts into our being. This brings change. There are always alternate explanations that we do not see, and Daniel learned how to see them.

Even though the hospital was a bad experience, we all walked out with the understanding that "we shared the universe, a universe we could feel within us."

Email from Washington:

We have decided to declare the entire group terrorists, an alien plot to take over the world. In this way we can seize their assets. Without money it may be a little harder for them to stay supplied with what is needed to feed the entire town. At the least they may think twice about bringing so many people to live in their town with them. We have forensic accountants working to identify exactly what they own. So far we have come up with a little over fifty billion dollars. Some of the companies we have been able to trace are held in stock which we can't touch, but we can intercept their dividend. We plan to take the stock into our special section and use the dividends to fund our operations. We may be getting a raise soon. :) If you have any Jewish operatives under your command keep them under surveillance. We think that Daniel and his group are a Jewish organization planted here centuries ago. So be watchful.

Email to Washington:

Thanks for the update. I'm looking forward to getting a raise. How much of the fifty billion do we get hold of? You don't have to worry about Jewish agents at this end, I got rid of them years ago. I knew from the get-go not to trust any Jew. I have for a long time pointed out how the aliens stop all activity on Friday night and Saturday. We have seen them light candles. And they pray. I always thought they were Jews. What's with all that do the right thing shit. Helping others so they can make money that's all it is. Just like all the Jews they make believe they are helping while they are only helping themselves. I knew the Jews were aliens before all this happened. Even when I was a kid growing up, I could tell. The little beanies they wear so they can identify one another. How secretive they are with those meeting they have on Saturdays. Fighting bleeding heart causes; the civil rights movement, the anti-war movement. Remember it was them that gave the Russians the atomic bomb. I knew all along they were aliens.

The outside world never ceased to amaze us. One day my mother said I should put the TV on. To my horror there was a panel discussing us. They said we were freaks and aliens plotting to take over the world. They said we actually preceded EL here to create the ridiculous story of the great lovable alien. Another person said we should be destroyed before we became too powerful. This reminded us of how isolated we were. We hoped EL would come soon. The TV panel was a clear demonstration of how fear had brought out the preachers of hate. It was really terrible to hear the hatred the outside world had for us.

Another program claimed we were a Jewish plot to take over the world. They said that Jews were actually aliens waiting for their mother ship to come. They pointed to the fact we do almost nothing on Friday nights or Saturday. Being with our families and playing sports, eating, dancing and just appreciating our lives was considered doing nothing. We shut down Friday night because we believe that everyone should set aside time to be with their families and friends and just be grateful they exist.

We see nothing wrong with just being grateful for our chance to be here and help others. The media presents crazy ideas and wraps it together under the name of truth. Because of the programs calling us a "Jewish Plot" in many places around the world Jewish people were attacked. It was really insane how people think they have the right to "defend" themselves against a threat that didn't exist. We reached out to all the Jewish communities and offered to bring them to our town. We eventually picked up many young people. But most of the communities accepted their situation and stayed where they were. All told, we received about two thousand young Jewish families.

Email to Washington:

You see they are Jews. In the last few weeks, they have brought thousands of Jews to their village. I mean thousands from all over the world. We must keep in mind, when they start their attack, we should be ready, in every city, to kill the male Jews so they can't join in on the attack.

Email from Washington:

You are right we must be ready. I have set up a special unit to identify every Jew in this country.

—10—

I GUESS I SHOULD MENTION GOD. Daniel says that "God is present throughout the universe. God is the force of good we feel and hold within us." Daniel says "to better understand the force we could read Spinoza, Pierre Teilhard De Chardin, and Martin Buber and others who wrote of the human experience in connection to the universal force." As for us, we feel the positive force and share the feeling through good deeds. We all feel the presence of the force, and accept there is no intervening god. There is only our responsibility to share the force by helping others. We believe our individual acts of caring and loving make the world a better place.

We believe in prayers and praying. We know when you move an object, any object, it effects the universe. The good anyone does, affects the entire universe. In this way praying enhances the universe which responds to the wave of positive thoughts.

Daniel says "our believing in the coming of EL is no different than believing in the coming of a deity. Though EL is tangible to us, our children have never seen him. They only have our stories, and the movie. As time goes by, the stories will grow. If we, who actually saw him die before he comes, the stories would become exaggerated and I (Daniel) would be elevated to the status of prophet, my comments would become sacred."

Daniel says "most people need to believe in a god because they do not believe in themselves. If they did believe in themselves, they would discover the god they search for." The presence of the force is everywhere. We must look inside ourselves and feel the love of the universe to be able to claim it as our own. In claiming it we make it available to others.

Daniel has mentioned many times how "human intelligence comes through the female." I asked Daniel if women are so smart why are they repressed in so many cultures? He said "it is not enough to be smart. Like all intelligent people it is only a measure of what is possible. Women instinctively surrender themselves to protect the future of the species. If they do not surrender, they are beaten into submission physically, verbally, and psychologically. Women are aware, but to protect the species they accept their limited place in society. When a woman speaks up, she is usually beaten and sexually assaulted, and sometimes killed. Being smart is not the same as knowing. A person who is smart has the ability to learn, but if they do not study or have the tools to look into themselves and find the awareness, they never learn how to feel the universe and the choices that come with awareness."

Daniel says "being smart is only a potential. Parents make a big mistake because they think because their kids are smart, they will do well. Smart means you can do well not that you *will* do well. A smart person can see their culture and figure out how it functions; they can understand faster than others. But if they don't read and study, if they do not learn about literature, nor are exposed to history, science, math etc. they never find their passion. They become a disappointment to themselves. A hollowness sets in. They are so marginalized they can't even see themselves.

"Without education an intelligent person becomes ordinary. They get up each day to reinvent and rediscover the simplest of thing, feelings, emotion, etc. To fully appreciate the simplest of things requires awareness of self. Realize if the wheel had to be invented by every person daily there would be no progress. The people who are not aware reinvent the wheel every day. Worst, when they see those who don't have to reinvent it, they hate them and want them destroyed."

Daniel points out how sad it is for a child, who is really intelligent, to receive no guidance from the parents because the parents accept the nonsense that smart kids don't have to study. All children, even smart ones, should be expected to work to their potential. They must be challenged and exposed to new ideas. Not bullied or pushed but led by sharing and by example.

In today's world the educated are linked through computers and are redefining reality. They are altering the cultural environment to align with human dignity through love and awareness of love. New-world people can feel the universe and are aware of their place in it. They experience it through love. Those that can't feel the love, hate those that do.

Daniel says our group is an advanced form of humanity. We function with simple motives: to "continuously further our knowledge, help as many people as we can, and enjoy life. Everyone should value those ideas."

The young must learn to understand themselves, what makes them happy? How to interact with others? What are the different forms of love and the relationships love creates? The young are vulnerable to outside influences which in many cases prevents them from developing. There are many pretenders exploiting the naivety of the young for their own gain and pleasure. That is why children must be protected.

For a child to become an adult they must accept their parents. They don't have to like their parents they must realize all parents do their best. Their best might really be disgusting, but that is all they knew. If a person hates their parents, they will never grow up. A person may not like what their parents did but they must accept that they gave them life. They acted within the limitations of their understanding. They might have caused pain but being alive gives choices. To pursue a happy life there must be acceptance of the parents. At the very least, they gave you life. Accepting the parents did their best, frees the person. They appreciate and celebrate the importance of "now." They learn to enjoy every moment. Those who dwell on the limitations that brought them to "now," (this moment), are never happy. Any vestige of discontent closes off the enjoyment of being in the present.

Daniel thinks EL had come to Earth before and had inserted ideas in the past which helped change man's perceptions, Daniel thinks because EL loved him, when EL held him to say goodbye, the touch changed something. Daniel was already linked to EL mentally, the touch linked Daniel to EL in a deeper way, a spiritual way. When, in the hospital, Daniel held us individually with his both hands on our temples, we became linked to Daniel and received the change.

The change is permanent in us and is inherited by our children. We are a new form of humanity. But we are no threat to anyone because we respect all life. It is the government that doesn't care about our peaceful intentions. They see us as a threat to their power. The government rules by fear and have made the general public afraid of us. Mankind must learn to demand that their governmnents work for the betterment of humanity. The problem is to demand anything requires an awareness of self that doesn't currently exist in the mass of the population. Governments use ignorance in their population to pit one group against another. It is very easy to hate. Those that hate can never see the beauty and love in the universe. Can never co-operate with others to advance their own learning. We wish it were otherwise, but it is not. There are many of us that feel the love.

One day Daniel said he was picking up a call for help coming from a woman in prison in Ohio. We got together to form a mental bond to listen to her call. She was obviously one of us but apparently a criminal. We quickly ignored the criminal title because the government called us criminals. We googled her case and discovered she was in prison for murdering her stepfather. She had grown up on a farm. Her real father died in Iraq. Her mother married an abusive man Dahlia (that's her name) claimed repeatedly sexually assaulted her. She testified since she was five her stepfather would come into her room, beat her, and sexually assault her. She said her mother had to have known. Her mother admitted almost every night her husband would go into Dahlia's room for at least an hour, but she figured he was their "helping" her with her school work. She was positive he loved Dahlia.

One day when Dahlia was sixteen, he attacked her, she could not recall what happened, but he went flying. Almost every bone in his body was broken. The prosecutor claimed she had planned the attack and charged her with first degree premeditated murder.

The district attorney pointed to the injuries found on the body, a small girl like Dahlia could never do so much damage to such a large man. She is five feet tall, 105 pounds. He was 6'3" tall 280 pounds. She had to have planned the attack "according to the evidence." There was no other explanation of how such a small girl could have destroyed such a large man. Even her own mother felt she probably planned it. Her mother testified Dahlia had never liked her stepfather, never gave him a chance. The trial ended with her convicted and sentenced to prison for life with no parole.

Daniel said "if we were threatened by real violence we would have to fight back." He pointed out what I did to protect myself and what had happened to my attacker at Harvard. Maybe she screamed? It seemed logical to us. A bigger question was how had she acquired the power? Is it possible mankind had arrived at that point in evolution without EL's intervention? Or maybe, when a change occurs it replicates itself in more than one place simultaneously? She was born during the time EL was on Earth. Dahlia's existence certainly raised a lot of questions.

We realized in an environment with no education it didn't matter if she was advanced. Dahlia may have the change, but it meant nothing. Repression could reduce the change to subservience. Daniel had each of us listen to Dahlia and evaluated what we heard. We concluded she was a good person full of love caught in the circumstances of bad choices in an environment with very few good opportunities.

What should we do? Should we rescue her? If yes, how? What we decided was very exciting to me because again I was chosen with four others to go to her aid. (actually, I picked myself). I was excited for several reasons, one I could help her, and two I was striking back at the system. We used our stealth planes and traveled to Ohio. Near the prison we shut down the electricity. Then we tuned in to Dahlia and told her to follow our instructions. We projected a force field around her and told her to concentrate on the lock on her cell door. When the cell door opened, she walked out, we told her where to turn and to concentrate on every door she encountered. She did exactly what we instructed. She walked out of her cell and proceeded to walk out of the prison.

The guards tried to grab her, and fired their weapons with no results. The bullets just bounced off. When she arrived at the main gate, I used a laser to disintegrate the twenty-foot high, large steel door. The guards were shocked to see this little girl walking toward them, they fired at her. The bullets bouncing back at them and many guards were wounded. The guards could not understand where the large steel door had gone. She just walked out to us. Quickly she boarded our plane and we took off. Once off the ground we restored the electricity and returned to California.

The next day we read about the "Ohio prison break." The story said Dahlia had lots of help escaping, thirty guards were shot, noncritically. The authorities were searching for her and her accomplices. She was considered armed and dangerous. The guards said there were at least a dozen accomplices with automatic weapons and a waiting aircraft, we just laughed at their imagination.

Back in California we assembled and listened to her story. She spoke of feeling strange her whole life and always trying to help people. She spoke of the beatings and the frequent sexual assaults. It was obvious she was one of us and we were glad we had rescued her. Her presence reawoke our concern for the safely of those outside of our town, and, of course, not having heard from EL. It had been many years since we started transmitting. We never expected so much time would pass. Daniel reassured us he would come.

Email from Washington:
We have been able to identify the team that broke into the Ohio prison and freed that murderer, it was that bitch Kate and some of her fellow aliens. Why they wanted her we can't figure out. Maybe they are assembling a team of assassins to retaliate against the world leaders? This could be the beginning of their move to take over the world. They probably want to create instability to weaken governments and thus weaken world cooperation. Keep the team ready. Try to figure out just what they are up to. As soon as we have a little more evidence, I will alert our state department to the possibility of this new threat. This is part of their bigger pattern of recruiting bodies to be used to take over.

We questioned her and quickly paired her with a mentor. Our social workers reach out to reduce the pain of what had happened to her at the hands of her stepfather and the adult inmates. She was placed in an education program and given a job. She graduated from our university with a PhD in psychology. It didn't take long for her to find a boyfriend and a girlfriend.

Her study of psychology was her need to explain to herself the meaning of the many variations of feelings she had experienced. Even though she knew she was free of the turmoil it still had a hold of her inner self. She had nightmares of the various and numerous attacks on her body and mind. We could see even with great intelligence the damage done by events and others had a very lasting effect. Her being bisexual was a natural outcome of the love for others she held. A love which she demonstrated through relationships.

She was grateful we had rescued her and had one request, in spite of how her mother treated her, she asked if we could send her mother an allowance to make her life a little better. Her mother was working as a waitress and rented a trailer. At Dahlia's request, we set up a trust that sent her a monthly check. We also bought her a house. As soon as the checks started coming, she quit her job and some guy moved in with her. Dahlia said that was how her mother saw herself and there was no way to change it.

Today Dahlia is married with nine children. She is one of our leading authorities on the effects of trauma on the mind.

We enjoy relationships. Not always in a sexual way but always in a loving and caring way. Daniel said "human relations, even sexual ones, should never be labeled." Sharing love with another human being is natural. When a person labels another being, they are saying the person is different from themselves. When a person labels themselves, they are limiting their own identity. Worse they are locking themselves in a form which represents the limitations of that moment in their lives. Reality is we are who we are, no more, no less. Each day changes us as does each experience. Daniel says "to the question, who are you? There is only one answer, I am who I am. A person is never their job, nor one of their roles in life, nor their relationships. A person is always their inner self, even if they cannot see it. If they can't feel who they are, they give themselves labels covering up their confusion. They remain in the limitation of the label and never search out their universal human identity, the who they are."

To share a life with another person is beautiful. If you look at society there are a mass of lonely people waiting for the magic of a relationship. What is so destructive to human life is the isolation experienced while being surrounded by others. Love can be seen but it is out of reach. In our group we touch and feel a lot, enjoy relationships, and constantly interact with each other. There is no time for anyone to be alone. We operate with a respect born of love for each other and the realization that loving one person adds to the positive force in the universe. Sharing your feelings with others is an act of love.

That having been said does not negate the fact that we are always alone within ourself. If you dwell on this it can be a very lonely experience. The key is to accept it as natural, accept you are alone inside yourself, but you share that in a spiritual way with the universe. Every one you know is "alone." Whether we are alone or not doesn't matter for we live life doing, helping others. This fills our "now" with love and purpose. A collection of happy "nows," filled with love and purpose, is the definition of a happy life.

Loving can also create problems. My daughter, Carol, met a boy named Sailor in first grade, a gifted student from outside our town. It may sound silly they fell in love. Even as little children it was so interesting to see their commonality. They were always together. He is smart and funny, loves telling jokes, Carol laughing all the time she was with him. He was not part of our group but he was educated in our schools and clearly shared our values.

They had remained friends throughout the years. Carol spent a lot of time at his home and he at ours. It was interesting to watch them. She is very aware of his feelings and she knows of his love through the mingling of their thoughts. The first time they kissed it was her initiative. They were standing facing each other she could hear his desire to kiss her so she casually leaned forward and they kissed. The most amazing thing happened. It was an awakening of the two spirits, they understood love.

Email to Washington:

I have a plan to capture Kate's daughter Carol. We figure she doesn't have the power that Daniel or her mother have. So, it might be possible to force her into a van and just drive away with her. I won't have the mother, but I'll have the daughter. I've assembled a team of physically very large men. It seems simple enough. We will drive up shove her into our van and drive away. Once we have her isolated, we can figure out how to get rid of that shield. We have a secure lock down ready. It cost a bundle but it has lead walls a foot thick, backed by a foot of steel, then concrete two feet thick. It is in a secluded location and we figure with those walls she will be unable to communicate with the outside. Let us keep our fingers crossed. If all goes well, we will have our first guinea pig. If we can't break through the shield, we can starve her then do our experiments. We are waiting for the right moment when she is by herself. I'll keep you informed.

Carol and Sailor went everywhere together, inseparable, holding hands, kissing. Other kids teased them; they didn't care. They planned to go to the same college. They remained very close, even after the government started attacking us.

One day, they had a date to go to a movie. While standing in front of Sailor's house holding hands, as usual enjoying the time together, unaware of the impending danger. The government decided to kidnap Carol. They had the idea they could just push her into a van.

A van pulled up alongside of them, four men jumped out and pushed Carol into the van. Sailor grabbed one of the men and hit him, but Sailor was thrown to the ground. His parents came out and tried to help. The government agents pushed them too. Carol was scared and screamed. The van shattered from the inside out. The three agents in the van died. The agent getting into the van was bleeding and lying on the ground. Carol got out and ran to Sailor. His father called the police and then called me. When the cops arrived, they questioned everyone.

Then, a large group of heavily armed federal agents arrived. Pulling out guns they tried to arrest Carol and me. When I tried to protect my daughter one of the agents fired at her but the bullets bounced off and hit another officer. Carol screamed again and all the federal agents were thrown against their cars and were badly hurt. The police stood there with their mouths opened. I told Carol we had to leave, she turned to Sailor's parents and apologized. They mumbled something to the effect they realized it wasn't her fault. Carol walked over and kissed Sailor. They held each other, crying. Then Carol and I got into our car and drove away.

Email to Washington:

Bad news. My team was able to successfully throw her into the van, she screamed and destroyed the van and killed the entire team. That's how her mother killed that innocent guy at Harvard. We sent in backup but by the time they arrived, her bitchy mother was there and terrorized the entire force. The backup team was killed. All toll we lost thirty-two men. We have it on video. A second backup team went in with the same results. Damn it, even their kids have powers. I can't understand why they haven't attacked us yet. With all that power and being untouchable it is difficult to understand. If we had half their abilities, we would rule the world. They must be waiting for a signal from outer space. They probably will attack when the mother ship arrives. That's when they will attack, I'm sure. In the meantime, we are working on other ideas. I'll keep you posted.

Sailor's parents were freaked out. They didn't blame Carol, but they were scared. Sailor and his parents were questioned by the police for hours and finally let go. The next day the newspapers had front page stories about how my daughter and I got into an argument with a "local family" and when the police were called, we "opened fire on the police and eighty officers were killed and ten others wounded." The editorial page called on the government to do something about the clear threat from the aliens. They identified us as Daniel's sister Kate and his niece. They had their headlines, "the women are more vicious than the men." We felt terrible, especially for Carol.

Sailor's family, because of what they witnessed, social pressure, and the portrayal of us as monsters, told Sailor not to see nor contact Carol. They had seen the power Carol had just screaming and they saw how bullets didn't touch us. Sailor's family loved Carol, but were scared. It was very difficult for them. Their friends wondered how they ever let their son go out with "an alien." But this didn't stop Sailor and Carol from getting together.

Sailor knew he was being watched but was still able to meet Carol. They hugged and kissed but mostly talked about their situation. He agreed to have a device implanted so they could communicate. Carol told him she could very easily do it and it wouldn't hurt. But she really didn't implant a device, she held his head in her hands and while kissing him she breathed us into him. He didn't realize it, and Carol didn't tell him. She also didn't tell us.

It had been thirty-nine years since EL was on Earth and twenty-five years since we began transmitting for help. We were worried we didn't expect so much time would go by without a response. We were in no danger and could hold out indefinitely, but it bothered us that so many people died attacking us.

I asked Daniel why they just kept attacking even though they could see it had no effect? Daniel said "very few governments learn from their mistakes. They repeat the same patterns over and over again. When a new government is elected, they always promise to reform the system. They take power then proceed to get rid of the old group, replacing it with their own friends. They almost never try to identify problems, let alone fix them."

All governments are only interested in power. The new government attacks the policies of the previous government and proceeds to prosecute the out of office former government official. This goes on until that government is replaced and the next group repeats the same pattern. They do nothing to improve the system because they define change as getting rid of the old players and their policies. That is why nothing changes no matter who takes office. Results do not matter because the definition of governing is opposing. What happens in a nation is never the fault of the ruling party. Whatever goes wrong is always the fault of the previous administration.

The government just kept attacking, this was the accepted method of demonstrating to their constituents they were doing something. "Politicians know very well how to oppose."

It was absolutely insane.

We were getting a discouraged waiting for EL. Daniel kept reassuring us he would come. I believed Daniel, but I was getting annoyed we were not defending ourselves. I kept arguing we had to do something, Daniel pointed out "none of us had been hurt. There was no need to use force on them. At least not now, Sis." That "not now, Sis" was really annoying.

We had a long discussion. Daniel was quiet while we looked for a way to teach the government a lesson. We wanted to do something about the lies the news media was spreading. We decided to override all radio and TV transmissions around the world and send a message of peace and love. (This wasn't my first choice.) We broadcast actual pictures of the government attacking us. Our images showed how the attack was getting nowhere, anyone could see we were not shooting back, in fact, you could see our kids playing. Daniel pointed out it was a "waste of human life" to attack us. "You can see it has no effect, your attacks will not change anything, it must be obvious that you can't touch us. Save your own lives and stop the stupidity of throwing young kids against us because you feel inadequate."

Daniel said "each person should evaluate their own behavior and try to understand their own motives for accepting the nonsense the media and the government say about us. You should ask yourself what harm had you actually seen committed by any of us? Did anyone you knew witness the lies the news media was spreading? We are being accused without proof." Daniel looked at the camera and said "you would not want to be attacked and have your children put in danger for no reason." Daniel told the audience they "should not do to others that which they would not want done to themselves. It should be everyone's goal to help humanity. Love was needed to overcome the hatred that is spread by the government and the press."

Email from Washington:

Did you see the arrogant son of a bitch threaten us? Who the hell does he think he is? He thinks we can do nothing to stop him? We are working on a plan that will be rolled out soon. By the way, isn't it great to have access to unlimited funds? The best part is that no one, not even the President, really knows we exist. They know I head the section on counter aliens, but who we employ and our methods fly under the radar. You have my approval to build another facility for yourself, make sure it has a pool and large guest rooms. You can call it a regional office. You also have my approval to build that retreat in the mountains. I thought the layout was stunning. Push the project so we have it for the summer. Remember we have unlimited funds and we might as well spend it.

The news media distorted what Daniel said. There were panel discussions dissecting every word. This was proof positive we intended to take over the planet. "You see how arrogantly Daniel laughed at the world saying there was nothing that could be done to stop him." The media said the battle scenes shown were a trick, we were showing a movie and not the actual attack taking place. There were discussions of how arrogant we all were. That was their new word for us "arrogant." They said, we intended to take over the earth with the help of alien spaceships.

Email to Washington:

Thanks for the OK on the buildings. I think Daniel going on TV backfired. The media is screaming for their blood. Now it is clear to everyone they are threatening all mankind. They are laughing at our inability to touch them. We are also working on a few ideas here. I hope to put at least one into play soon. I'll run it by you when all details are in place. I know you said I can act on my own, but your input is very valuable. We want things to be done right. Again thanks. Having money certainly increases our ability to find solutions.

While the news media was condemning us, we received over forty million emails messages of love and hope from all over the world. It was satisfying to know so many people understood and accepted us.

Daniel said "the change was coming anyway no matter what the government might do. It might take longer, much longer if the governments shut down the internet. But it was coming. The young see the hypocrisy of governments supporting programs aimed at helping the wealthy and not the working class. Individuals who achieve new-world consciousness know governments should always serve the good of the people."

Daniel said the "wealthy were to blame. They are greedy. They would do much better if they shared a little more and gave workers a real living wage. The workers would be able to spend on the products that would support the investments of the wealthy."

—11—

TIRED OF ALL THE ATTACKS, it was suggested we could use some of the offensive weapons (I wonder who suggested that? Smile). Our main concern was to insure no one was hurt. Our engineers perfected destructive weapons just in case we might need them. Many were discovered while doing research on unrelated ideas, like the various uses for a laser.

It was decided we could use our lasers to eliminate some of the military equipment. Our lasers could disintegrate anything from twenty miles away. We examined satellite images and watched the troops to establish a pattern. Nightly the equipment was parked unoccupied in various locations. We selected one target to see what reaction we might get.

Our first target was a tank depot. There were twelve tanks parked very close to each other. The two guards were more than sixty feet away in a small hut. Our lasers were placed aboard one of our planes. When we hit the tanks, they turned into dust. We carefully monitored the military frequencies the next day. It was so funny to hear them questioning everyone about where the tanks had been put? Could they have been stolen? Who could have stolen them? Were they sure of the location? Why are they not there? Why didn't anyone see them moved? They had surveillance video they kept looking at over and over again. They could see the tanks, then in an instant they were gone. They kept saying someone had doctored the video. Over the next few weeks all the tanks, the artillery, the trucks, the cars, and several storage buildings all disappeared. The soldiers were lucky to still have their rifles, but they had very little ammunition. One of the storage building was their ammunitions site. (smile)

It was so much fun watching and listening to the debate. We broadcast the event live to our whole town. This was such a great success, we picked other targets. In each case it was the same. Just for a joke we picked a Navy destroyer in dry dock. The workers showed up and found no ship. It was so great to listen to and watch. We could hear them being questioned. Important persons flew in from Washington. We just laughed for hours.

Email from Washington:

What the hell is going on out there? The military is saying they have lost all their equipment and supplies. They even said they have lost all the ammunition that was stored out there including the building it was in. What gives? Are they attacking? We knew they would, but how?

Email to Washington:

It is true, every last piece of equipment and the storage facilities have completely disappeared. I know it's them, but I can't figure out how they are pulling it off. There is no sign of any movement in their town. We see them laughing a lot but what that means I don't know. Even replacement vehicles disappear as soon as they are brought in. I'm at a loss as to what to do. We certainly can't admit publicly that they are defeating us. But I am sure they are behind this whole mess. For now, I think we should back off before they decide to take us out.

Oh! I guess I should explain what our lasers did or rather what the workers found, NOTHING. The ship was turned to dust. No one figured the dust was the remains of the ship. We laughed for days while hunting for new targets. Not just to slow up the government's ability to attack us, but also for the comedy show we were treated to. It was great fun. We accessed cameras in the areas to enjoy the expressions on the faces. Sensors picked up all the voices. We could actually use any existing phone or computer to listen and see what was going on.

We found great targets. The head of the Joint Chiefs of Staff, (he runs the entire military), he parked his new Mercedes outside a Home Depot. When his driver walked away from the car to help the general, "zap" the car was gone. We just laughed at the expression on their faces and the comments.

We realized the government was getting the message we could and would fight back. So we looked for a really good target, one that would be the funniest. Everyone laughed as new ideas were presented. One person suggested we zap Disneyland, but that was vetoed because our kids love going there. Another thought we could make a bridge like the Golden Gate disappear. Or how about a building? The Pentagon? It was great fun just deciding what to do next.

We decide to eliminate the Washington Monument the day before George Washington's birthday, there were many festivities planned. That night we zapped (I love that word) the monument. The next day a large crowd gathered, there was no obelisk. We were hysterical with laughter. The politicians were beside themselves. They couldn't say we did it, it would be an admission of failure and a public demonstration of our powers. The story was there had been an earthquake, the monument fell, and the government had it cleaned up quickly for the ceremonies. The politicians pledged to build a new one. But we achieved our objective. The government stopped attacking us. We could wait for EL in peace.

But it had become a great game to us. With each zap we would laugh. So we continued.

We zapped empty buildings.

We zapped an old railroad bridge.

We zapped a stadium. There was this abandoned stadium and no one could decide whether to fix or tear down, so we zapped it. It was so much fun.

We zapped a senator's car. (the one who had called Daniel a "son of a bitch.")

OH! We zapped the right side of the CIA headquarters in Virginia were the director had his office.

I guess I should add that for many years we had recorded every use of phones, every use of the internet in the world, all emails, all cameras. We could actually tune into a specific car radio and listen to the conversation of the occupants. So it was no big deal for us to enjoy the interchange when the director of the CIA arrived at his office to find the hall ended just before his office door. He could see the parking lot outside. The cut was perfect with no ragged edges, (smile), we loved it.

Email from Washington:

You were right they were behind the disappearance of those tanks and all the military equipment. We now know all of the attacks are coming from them. We cannot allow the press to print a word of it. We have decided to stop overtly attacking them for now. If we get an opening or a great idea, we will implement it. Actually, it was really funny to see the director of the CIA put in such a funny situation. He kept saying, "My golf clubs were in my office." That's good for that bastard. He has always hated me and is jealous of my position. He can't understand why the hell we have pursued our attacks all these years against the aliens. He keeps telling the President "there is no evidence they are aliens. There is no evidence they have ever attacked anyone. There is a great deal of evidence they have worked to improve the conditions of all mankind." He points out with all the power at their disposal, they have not deliberately hurt anyone. I have heard from friends he calls you and me "two jerks with an agenda based on ignorance." Now who's laughing? Where are his fucking golf clubs?

Email to Washington:

Yes, it was fairly obvious they are disintegrating objects at will all over the place, we haven't figured out how they do it. It must be some kind of lasers. I agree all attacks against them should stop. With this weapon we are all very vulnerable. They may become more aggressive and take out some of us. They certainly have the ability. I would have loved to see the director's face when he found his office gone. The best part is he lost his "golf clubs." That's good for the son of a bitch. He should have been in his office when they took it out. I didn't know he hated us so. He and people like him are just the reason it took us so long to show the rest of the world the real nature of those aliens. We should make a list of our enemies and use our assets to eliminate them. They are endangering mankind. If we can't get the aliens, we can get their sympathizers. Imagine if we had that weapon? We could rule the world.

–12–

W E WENT FREQUENTLY TO NEW YORK CITY. It was Mitch and Ebana who originally introduced us to the great cultural events of the city. What we loved most about it was the anonymity. No one seems to care who we were. They rush about their business leaving everyone alone. Even once or twice when someone did recognize us, they just said hi and went about their day. There was this one guy that looked at Daniel and said "you don't look like an alien" and kept on walking. On a couple occasion we were asked for autographs. For the most part we could go out to dine and to the theater without any problems. There are great restaurants and the owners guarantee privacy,

We were in New York for a few reasons. For one we wanted to attend a lecture at Columbia University. We also had tickets to the opening of a new play. It was a happy occasion for us. Daniel, Paige, Vinny, and me planned to meet Mitch and Ebana for dinner. Ebana and her family are from New York so they were busy with her relatives. At the time Ebana was beginning her ninth month of pregnancy.

After the lecture, the four of us went to the Statue of Liberty. I had never been there so it was a treat. The others loved teasing me about things I hadn't done, starting with flying on the bicycles and they never missed an opportunity to say "you mean you never." While we were at the statue, we all felt a horror pass through our bodies.

Mitch and Ebana were in a car accident on their way to their Midtown apartment. Neither of them were hurt, but Ebana started having labor pains so an ambulance took them to the hospital. The horror we experienced was Mitchell's death. We learned later Mitch was excited and was handed a cup of coffee. It was poisoned and he died.

Email to Washington:

We got one. We just killed Daniel's brother Mitchell. We were lucky our team was following them when they were involved in an accident and taken to the hospital. They weren't hurt. It was his wife who needed assistance. She is pregnant and started having contractions. One of our team inserted herself into the scene and gave Mitch a poisoned cup of coffee, which he drank. We have his body in a special room. He has no shield. Apparently, the shield is controlled by his mind. They have taken blood samples and x-rays but have done no further testing awaiting our team of specialists to fly in. They have already arrived in New York and are stuck in traffic. His wife we have isolated. It looks like she will give birth any minute then we will have one dead and two live specimens to work on. I have positioned around the hospital eight thousand armed men. That will hold them. I'll keep you posted.

Email from Washington:

Great news. I await your follow-up. By the way, I know it's not the one you want, but you can have that Ebana. After we are finished with her, of course, provided you like black meat? Whoever poisoned him should be promoted and get a substantial raise. We have been waiting for a chance like this. Do you think their babies are born with a protective shield? We will soon find out. I'm so happy. We will have our proof. I'm almost tempted to fly to New York to be there for this great moment. Keep me posted.

As we felt the horror Daniel said, "Let's go. We walked to the edge of the pier on Liberty Island and the four of us lifted off the ground flying in front of about a thousand people. We headed toward the distress signal coming from Ebana. As we arrived, we confronted an enormous number of armed personnel with heavy weapons and armored vehicles. Daniel looked at me and said, "NOW SIS! NOW!

They never knew what hit them. I had been waiting for this chance and I made the best of it. Outside the hospital were armored vehicles and at least three thousand armed men. Daniel walking behind the three of us. Me blasting away with my trusty laser, (not the disintegrator), Paige and Vinny throwing fire balls and bolts of electricity as we walked forward. We walked into the lobby with all the fools running for cover to avoid my laser and the fire balls. Daniel told Vinny and Paige to get Ebana. While he and I walked into an elevator pressed the floor where they were holding Mitch's body. They shut down the elevator. We moved it with our minds. Upon arriving at the floor, we again encountered more armed men. I didn't wait for Daniel to say a word, I hit them with everything I had. I blew open the door to the room where Mitch was and we walked in. A few idiots aimed their weapons at us; I blew them away. There were at least ten doctors, I assume they were doctors, both male and female wearing white coats standing there. They didn't move. Daniel, with tears in his eyes, walked over and hugged Mitchell. As he did so you could see Mitch's eyes open. He looked at Daniel and said, "How are Ebana and the baby?"

The three of us walked out of the hospital. Paige and Vinny had Ebana and the baby. Outside I continued destroying all the vehicles in the parking lot. I even destroyed the garage in which thousands of men were shooting at us. Daniel looked at me, so I stopped. The seven of us took an ambulance abandoned by the driver when he saw us coming. Before we got into the ambulance there was a hot dog cart near the ambulance, Daniel said "get all the water on the cart" we used it to clean out Mitchell's system. I left a thousand dollars for the owner. We immediately drove to the airport and returned to California.

Email to Washington:

We lost them all. They just walked into the hospital, killed more than half my team and some innocent bystanders. People who were not bothering them. You should have seen how their king, Daniel just walked behind his sister, his wife and his sister's husband and did nothing. They cleared the path by destroying and killing innocent people. He just walked straight ahead while they did his dirty work. They got into an elevator that had no electricity and it rose up and took them to the exact floor where we were holding the body. There I lost another three hundred men. Paige and Vinny went to get Ebana and the baby while Daniel and Kate went to get Mitchell. They just walked into the room where the body was, and that alien brought his brother back to life. The doctors who witnessed it said Daniel hugged his brother and just like that Mitchell opened his eyes and asked about his wife and child. The doctors said that the men we had in the room guarding the body were killed by Kate. As they were leaving the floor that bitch Kate destroyed everything in sight. There is a large gaping hole in the side of the building

Email to Washington. continued:

They destroyed much of the facility. Destroyed hundreds of cars in the parking lot. She demolished a six-story garage. I mean this garage that occupied a whole city block and held about ten thousand cars was left completely collapsed. We had about a thousand men in the garage. And there were hundreds of innocent people. Most of the destruction was caused by Kate. You should have seen it. I was there and couldn't believe she was firing some kind of a laser while her husband and Daniel's wife were hurling fire balls and lightning bolts at every one. With that much power it is a wonder they haven't taken over the planet already. They just walked in and then they walked out leaving the place destroyed. As they were leaving, they must have been thirsty because they stole a case of water from a hot dog vendor. They also stole a city ambulance and drove it to the airport. On the highway they destroyed every obstacle we put in their path. About one hundred police cars among them. We knew where they were going and had a small army waiting, but they just blew them away. Why would they do something like that? They have no regard for human life. They killed a lot of innocent people. They are just vicious.

Email from Washington:

Did I understand you correctly, Daniel brought his brother back to life? They just walked in and destroyed an entire facility for no reason? They are becoming more aggressive. They are probably almost ready to attack. Obviously, they are waiting for someone or something, probably their spaceship. You are right, with that kind of power they could do anything they want. The world is fortunate that we have held them at bay. We will never really get credit, but we know what we have accomplished. Your report said you lost over four thousand personnel. I hope they weren't our main force. I would hate to lose our elite group after all the special training we paid for. How many vehicles did you lose? Get me a complete report with exact numbers so I can put in a request for replacements. This should shut up the CIA director and his complaint about losing golf clubs. Fuck him. There is the proof of how vicious they are. This is just another four thousand to add to the list of good people they have killed for no reason. I will give the story to the press.

The press was all over the story. "According to unidentified government sources, Daniel's sister-in-law went into labor while visiting New York. She was taken to Bellevue Hospital and was unsatisfied with the attention she was getting. When Daniel and his sister arrived, they went crazy and destroyed the place killing over four thousand innocent people, patients, and employees of the hospital. Everyone can see an enormous hole in the side of the building. On the way out they destroyed the parking garage which occupies an entire city block there were over ten thousand cars in the six-story garage. Many innocent patients and employees were killed by its destruction. As they left, they stole food and water from a hot dog vendor outside the hospital. The police gave chase, but the alien destroyed about three hundred police vehicles. At the airport they killed another two hundred TSA personnel. It is hard to believe that the government as allowed this kind of destruction to go on. This is not the first time they attacked innocent people."

"In a related story more than two thousand visitors to the Statue of Liberty were frightened by the aliens when they decided they were in a hurry to leave and instead of waiting for the boat they just lifted off the island, they went to the end of the pier and started flying, like Superman. The witnesses said they were really scared. Especially the way the aliens just pushed everyone out of the way when they decided to leave. One little girl was hurt but not seriously."

After the attack on Mitchell, we were left alone for a number of years. Apparently, they were at a loss as to what to do. My view is we scared the hell out of them. We should have done it sooner.

—13—

On a beautiful summer morning in July, the 4th to be exact, we received a message from outer space. Our whole town was happy. It said "EL is coming home." We were very sure the government knew we were contacted, the next day they began their stupid attacks all over again.

Email from Washington:

They have received a message from outer space. Our scientists say the signal is coming from within our solar system. So their space ship is coming. We knew it! We were right, they were waiting for reinforcements. We don't plan to go down without a fight. I briefed the President with this clear evidence that the alien's allies are on the way to Earth. That fuck from the CIA kept saying "how did we know they were coming to hurt us? If they had wanted to attack us, with all the power we know they have they would have already." But I convinced the President that we can't take a chance. They have to know we just won't be pushed over. If we go down, we should go down fighting. The President has ordered all our resources to be thrown at them. Good luck.

It was crazy, we watched as their tanks and bombs melted against our shields. On the television and in the newspapers they carried stories about how we were attacking. "The government holding off the aliens," read the headlines. We felt sad to see all those people die. Anyone with eyes could see we were in our town going about our daily lives. We even went to our perimeter and waved to the soldiers and cameras. What they could not see was how happy we were, we knew EL was coming.

The newspapers and television kept up a story that we were attacking and the government was "defending America." They said all mankind should be prepared to fight, our fellow "aliens were coming from outer space." This brought attacks all over the world on people who were smart and or lived helping others. A very large group of good, ordinary Americans we could see joining the attacks on us. They made camps a few miles from our town and carried guns and lots of American flags. Every once in a while, they would shoot at us, like when we waved hello. It was really dumb. Nothing hit us, but they just kept shooting. The bullets bounced back and hit them. It was mindless. How could they not realize they were being shot by their own bullets? They just kept shooting. Why would anyone continue a pattern so self destructive? Daniel said "there are so many examples of this ridiculous behavior: young people who smoke, people who drink in excess, people who drive without paying attention to the road, this was just another one for the list."

We received a second message, "we will be with you shortly. Prepare for our arrival." The message said if we wanted, they would take us to another planet." They explained it was very far from Earth and there would be no possibility of returning. We were sent data about the planet with photos of the land and animals. We were so happy. But it was a big decision. The message explained they could do nothing about the rest of humanity. They were coming to rescue us and could see why we called for help.

Daniel called us together, presented what options we had. It came down to three: we could take over the earth, we could stay where we were, or we could, as EL had suggested, leave the planet for a new world.

Daniel said "once a culture was no longer dominate it was doomed to die. Because we exist, they no longer could explain their place in the universe, they lose their purpose for living. Their answers to the meaning of life were no longer valid. Unable to eliminate us, the culture with the wrong answers turns on itself. One group tries to kill another. One group would claim to have the answer and would develop a following then they would splinter into other groups and attack each other. Their answers have no meaning so long as we exist, and there was no way of eliminating us."

Daniel pointed out "if we left the earth, we would become humanities higher purpose. We would become their legends. They would write books explaining our 'divine being.' That would give them purpose to live. Probably a religion would develop in our memory." I jokingly said Danielanity or Danielism, everyone laughed.

It was very obvious we would have to leave. It was a sad decision because this was our home. I was born in California. California was where I grew up. Our children loved Disneyland and the beaches. When you think about "home" you feel safe to be where others shared your growing up, where your children shared common memories.

This was not an easy choice. There was a great deal of crying. Memories were spoken of bringing all of us to tears. Places connected to our lives and loved ones. Sometimes silly things like Ebana spoke of Coney Island in Brooklyn, New York where her father took her as a child. Over the years since her father's death, she had gone there many times to realize the experience of being with him again. In fact, she and Mitchell had taken their own kids there. Practically everyone had similar attachment to some location, some special place where their being was touched. After a long session of tears and laughter, we realized we had no choice—we had to leave. We told everyone that if they wanted to invite their families to come, they could, but make it very clear they would never be able to come back. They also understood we maintained our policy of not accepting anyone who we could feel was evil or destructive.

Our decision was immediately transmitted to EL. In reply we received more pictures of where we were going and tons of data. That is when Carol came to me and said "she wanted Sailor to come." We said we would contact him and see if he was willing to leave with us. She then revealed that they were in constant contact because she had changed him. We were annoyed with her and she knew it, but what was done was done. We told her to invite him and his family. She was so happy.

Email to Washington:

We have been paralyzed by some kind of an electronic signal from their mother ship; now that we cannot attack they will simply destroy us. Do you think they may be cannibals? Remember that movie where the aliens were harvesting humanity for food? I'm a little scared, but I still have small arms and a large contingent ready to do battle. One crazy thing that is going on, you should see all the preachers declaring this is Armageddon. The world will end and God will sit in judgment. I wish they would shut up and just pick up a gun and fight instead of accepting their fate. They are so annoying with their seeing something that isn't there. They go on and on about "god is coming" NO! aliens are coming. You should see the size of their space ship. It's not even here yet and you can see it is enormous.

Email from Washington:

The President now sees how we were right. They were waiting for their mother ship. We don't know what to expect. They may be cannibals, who knows? The entire National Guard has been called up to be ready for when the aliens make their move. Keep me informed of what you can see happening inside their fortress. The Hubble Telescope has been turned to see the ship. You are right it is gigantic. They probably have a few divisions on board just itching to attack. But we are as ready as we can be. May God protect us.

The government kept attacking us. We were in no danger, but it was sad. Then it all stopped. One minute weapons were firing, the next it all just stopped. We guessed that EL had turned off the power sources operating the equipment. Their vehicles stopped working. Everything just froze in place. It was so strange to look out at the confusion. The soldiers were running all over the place giving orders, taking orders. You could see them trying to fix their equipment. I could not understand why it never dawned on them they could do nothing. You could see none of the equipment was working. I mean none. Their cars didn't work. They opened the hoods and looked in trying to figure out what was wrong. We just laughed.

While we were looking out at the inactive military equipment, a very large space ship appeared over our town. It was round with spotted lights and a bright beam coming from the center. It hovered above us. Then we saw a small vessel come out from the bright beam. We recognized it immediately, it was EL's ship.

Email to Washington:

Are you receiving the image of the enormous space ship that is hovering over their town? I can't believe it. It must be ten miles across. If there was any doubt as to their intentions, now it is clear. Their leaders have arrived. We should move the President into hiding in order to protect the authority of our democracy and laws. We know how ruthless these aliens are, but we might survive. Some of us might. I have already stashed supplies in the Rocky Mountains in various locations so that we can continue the battle as long as possible. I, for one, will never surrender.

Slowly EL's ship landed, the door opened and a platform deployed, there he was, EL. Daniel was the first to reach him. Daniel ran to him like a little boy calling his name "EL! EL!" We all stayed back with tears in our eyes. It was Daniel's moment. They hugged and both cried, it was wonderful. He walked over to me and Mitch and hugged us both. EL's friends came out of the ship and we all hugged. What a pleasure and relief it was after the years of tension, the attacks and the uncertainty of waiting for EL without really knowing if he would come. The hope EL would come fading as the years went by. Daniel always reassuring us. All the hatred for us and the attacks. The waste of lives. We cried with relief. EL was here at last.

The first thing EL asked was if we had any M&Ms. We all laughed. We did and gave them to him and he shared them with his mates. He explained they were all very excited to finally get to taste them. EL had told so many stories about the great food we gave him, that his ship was full of volunteers who came down to be the first to taste it. We all laughed.

Email to Washington:

I guess you can see all of our equipment has ceased to func-tion. In addition, a very large space ship has placed itself above the town. We have seen a number of smaller ships coming out of the mother ship and landing. There is our proof they are aliens. They were just waiting for the rest of their army. I have been busy organizing small groups with auto-matic weapons to be ready when they start the attack. For now, as far as we can tell they are just celebrating.

Our town gathered to listen to EL. He told us they were about five light years away when they received our signal. He was called to his Elders to explain what it meant. They recognized the signal as the same message EL had sent when he was stranded on Earth. EL immediately realized Daniel was calling for help. That is when he explained to his Elders how he had left Daniel with the power to defend himself by implanting his universal seed in Daniel. His Elders were annoyed with him, but they had already heard of how advanced Daniel was mentally and were grateful to Daniel and his family for saving EL. After a brief discussion they agreed to come and help as quickly as possible. It was the opinion of the Elders Daniel would be safe until they arrived.

The Elders ordered their crew to look around the universe for a new planet for Daniel. They had no idea if there was more than Daniel and his family to rescue, but they would have a planet picked out just in case. The worst-case scenario Daniel and his family would become members of their crew.   EL told us the new planet was much like Earth. There was life there but no high intelligence. There were plenty of resources and with our knowledge and technology it would not be long before we would be settled.

This was a beautiful moment, a completion of our hopes and dreams. EL spoke about Daniel and our family and how we had saved him. "They took me in and truly loved me." He said he and his people felt privileged to come to rescue us.

When he finished, Daniel addressed the group. "I wish I could guaranty we will be okay. I believe we will do well. We have a great deal of knowledge, a good work ethic, and of course EL's help. Realize we can't stay here unless we take the offensive. That would mean a great many deaths. Not ours but still it would not be worth it. The rest of humanity thinks we are aliens and will never stop attacking us."

"You have a choice; if any of you want to stay on Earth, you can, but you would have to disappear into the general population and live without being noticed, without our technology. We will dismantle what we have created when we leave. We will erase your memory of what we built. If you are one of us with powers, I will remove any powers from your being. The government will probably mount a witch hunt much like what Senator Joseph McCarthy did in the 1950s. Who knows? They may kill all the children. They will certainly kill many intelligent people. They will arrest those who have helped the poor. They might even kill them. The nature of the backlash will be anti-intellectual. If you stay, we can't help you, EL has made that clear. We will not be back and we will be too far from Earth to be able to help.

"There is another danger if you stay, your children may evolve to be an emergence of new-world consciousness. The problem will start all over again and they will probably be killed, at least the men.

"You must decide within two weeks whether you want to stay or leave. One other point; as we know there are a number of people like us in the general population, we will pick up all who want to come with us. If any member of your family wishes to join us, we will pick them up too. There are also some who are unaware of the potential or connection to us. We cannot help them. For the most part they are safe. They will evolve normally. Our powers were derived from direct contact with EL. Even though they will be intelligent and will evolve quickly, the powers are genetic changes, our children naturally inherit them. Those who are left behind will have none of the powers. We will not permit any of you to retain the change if you decide to stay. The decision to stay or leave is yours and yours alone."

Everyone decided to leave. There was only one problem: Sailor. He had not answered Carol. She was very upset but could do nothing. It was his decision not hers.

EL asked how many people would be going on the journey? Daniel estimated we were just over thirty thousand living in our town. And there were pockets of people all around the globe. Some might want to come. I mentioned Sailor and his family. Carol was happy I did. She had no idea what he and his family would do. EL said we should communicate with those outside and arrange to pick them up. They, of course, had to be careful. If it was realized they were going to join us, we were sure they would be killed. The method we used was simple. El had small space ships sent to various locations around the world. The ships sat on the ground with no movement at all. Very large crowds gathered to look. Our people simply blended in. Once we recognized them it was a simple matter to allow them to walk through our shield. We eventually picked up another five thousand families. About another two thousand families simply came to our border and requested asylum. We screened them carefully and admitted almost all.

EL was invited with his friends to dinner at my mother's house, but we quickly realized it would have to be moved to the main dining room in our college. We did stop at the house with EL for old times' sake. My mother was there with Kiel, me, Daniel, Mitch my father, all the kids from the hospital, all the spouses with all their kids. Everyone went outside while EL, my mother, Daniel, Mitchell, and me walked through the house crying.

At dinner EL told us his group had visited the earth many times in the past two hundred thousand years. On a few occasions they interacted with people. He explained because of the level of knowledge of the beings encountered, most were scared and ran away. A couple of times he encountered interesting individuals and shared concepts with them. He told the story of an individual to whom he spoke. One night, about four thousand years ago, EL was on top of a mountain when he encountered this lone human being. EL was carrying a bright light and kept it pointed at the eyes of the person. That person never really saw EL. He just heard his voice behind the bright light. But again the person, because of his limitation, could not fully understand what EL was explaining to him. He understood his way, with the limited vocabulary of his times.

Limitation or not, EL said the man was a very interesting person. He was curious about what rules could be developed to help his people. EL suggested a few and even wrote them down. Centuries later on a return visit, EL was pleased to find the rules still in use. The people had developed stories and cults around what they understood. Some people actually expanded the rules. Each time EL had visited Earth he noted much progress. The rules had introduced morality into human consciousness.

EL said the last time he had visited Earth, with almost disastrous consequences, he was emotionally overwhelmed by the love he received from Daniel and the acceptance by his family. But the most extraordinary thing was how Daniel melded mentally with him. EL had never encountered a complete mental interaction with any other human. He realized the human race had truly advanced. He was amazed at how Daniel, his family and friends risked their lives to save him. EL knew this evolved human, Daniel, was ready to receive the inner understanding of the universe. It was amazing to EL, since his last visit, mankind had become so advanced. When he was rescued and reached his ship, he anxiously told his Elders. They too were excited by this advancement in humanity.

EL explained to his Elders when he hugged Daniel they became one. Daniel had evolved to a state where love was conscious. This is why he could bind mentally with him. When EL said goodbye to Daniel and hugged him, he enhanced Daniel's mutation to put Daniel in contact with all knowledge. He did not realize Daniel would be able to transfer the change. EL had no idea so many people had evolved around the world. Even more, EL did not know humanity had developed to the point where global culture was emerging. He never thought Daniel's touch would bring about the replication of the genetic change in others.

EL meant only to protect Daniel whom he loved so much, like you protect your own child. He wanted Daniel to be safe. He did not think increased intelligence would be such a threat to humanity. But as EL and his Elders approached Earth and saw the hatred directed against Daniel and his family, EL felt vindicated he had given Daniel the ability to protect himself, and so did his Elders. EL said, Daniel and his family were already a new evolved form of humanity, he only made Daniel less vulnerable.

Email from Washington:
_____
What are they waiting for now?

Email to Washington:
_____
It beats me. I have no idea why they haven't started the attack. They seem to be celebrating. Many of their space buddies are at a dinner in their college. They must be telling the stories of how we have tried to stop them. They are probably gloating.

We were extended an invitation to visit the main spaceship. It was amazingly big. There was an entire section with hundreds of small ships like EL used. There were thousands of ELs on board and other races. They came out to see us, many just walked over and hugged us and we could feel them connecting with us mentally. It was just wonderful, a feeling of coming home.

The ship was enormous. Two hundred of us had came up with EL on his "small" ship. EL explained the mother ship was an explorer ship used to travel the universe. The small ships brought explorers to the surface of planets. He noted the large explorer usually never comes close to a planet. It remained a long distance away so as not to be visible. There were many voyagers from many planets on board. They represented species that had evolved to universal love and thus understood and embodied the universe. They all traveled the universe cataloging the planets and noting the changes since their last visit.

We were taken to an assembly area where we were introduced to a large group, Daniel was asked to speak. Daniel looked at the audience and thanked them for coming to our rescue. He expressed our gratitude for all that was offered and pledged we would do our best to achieve what was expected of us.

Email to Washington:

They are making a move. Their entire high command has boarded a space ship and have been transported to the mother ship. I am positive they are meeting with the generals on board to plan their attack. They are probably receiving the weapons they need to attack us simultaneously all over the world. I'm sure from the way they reproduce they are going to round up many beautiful women and bring them as an offering to the crew of the mother ship. Kate went up with the group she is probably right now giving them a lesson in aggressiveness. I am all ready for them. I'll keep you posted.

When Daniel stopped speaking, a person similar to EL came forward. Everyone got very quiet. He said his name was Yashi and he welcomed us. He told us EL had been admonished for interfering in the evolution of humanity. It was not their mission to interfere in a planet's development. But now that he has met us, he could understand why EL did what he did. Yashi explained it takes tens of thousands of years for an intelligent species to come to understand the power of love. Such a journey is difficult. Usually when an individual did achieve it, he or she was destroyed. Yashi said it was obvious we had made the journey successfully. Yashi could see our connection to the universe through love.

Yashi said Daniel and his people would have survived and could never have been defeated. He pointed out, what Daniel had already explained, a group that evolved within a species the way we did is a threat to the existence of the old model. Many evolved prototypes do not survive. But when they do, they eventually take over. He said EL had done the right thing to enhance our development so that we could protect ourselves.

Yashi said this was the first time in a half a million earth years they have come to intervene in the natural development of a planet. They came because of the love EL had received from Daniel, his family, and friends, an unquestioning love that only sought to protect EL.

Yashi said because of our powers it was obvious we would have eventually replaced the rest of humanity. He was happy to welcome us to the universal family. Yashi walked over and hugged Daniel. Everyone applauded.

After we left the assembly EL and Yashi took us to a large room. EL explained this room was where the Elders met. When we walked in, Yashi went up and sat in the center chair. EL introduced us to his Elders. There were nine of them, YASHI, SHEK, YADI, ASEM, YA, ASHER, BAL, ROE, and SHADY. You could see they were from different species. They sat behind a semicircle and wore interesting hats. A six-pointed star worn around their necks. They said the star represented traveling to all the corners of the universe. We were served refreshments. They were truly curious about us. At one point one of the Elders turned to EL and said "I see why you love them." At that moment I realized we were talking to them and understood them with no difficulty. We simply understood their language.

They asked about the time we spent with EL. We told them how EL was dying and we could do nothing and how that hurt us so much, and what happened to us after he left. How we were taken to a hospital and for eight months were questioned. They all laughed when we told them the government believed we had summoned EL, and they were sure we were aliens placed on Earth to take over the planet.

We told them of the many projects we started all over the world. They were pleased with our accomplishments and said so. For a while they discussed how we had lowered the level of the oceans. One of them got all excited about the large trench we dug in the Sahara Dessert. Yashi laughed and said "can you tell her passion is civil engineering." We all joined in laughing. They assured us we would do well on our new planet, and pledged their support and help. One of them asked how we were able to contact them? We explained we used the device EL had used. They really enjoyed hearing our stories, while showing a great deal of concern about the behavior of the rest of humanity. Even entering into a discussion among themselves about the motives for the hatred comparing it to past events. You could see they were enjoying us and were happy they had come to our rescue.

We were invited to stay overnight; the Elders would see us at dinner. EL and some of his friends came to take us to our quarters. They showed us where our 40,000 plus fellow voyagers would be housed for the long journey. It was amazing how big the ship was. There were actually transporters used to move from one section to another, platforms you stepped on and requested a destination. They moved smoothly without any obvious source of power. When we asked how it ran, we were told it used magnetic transfer coils interacting with gravity generated on the ship.

We were very pleasantly surprised by the spacious quarters, the area was sectioned so every family would have their own living quarters with kitchens, bedrooms, dayrooms, bathrooms. We also had our own central kitchen. There was ample space for our schoolrooms and an area for recreation. There was a very large library which excited us very much.

The next day we continued the interview with the Elders. One of them asked why we thought the governments were so aggressive? Daniel pointed out though we only meant well and were doing good work, the establishment figured we were a threat because of how successful we were. We were a group working for the good of humanity and the government could not control us, so we became the outcasts and had to be eliminated.

The Elders said that was a kind view. They pointed out if they had not come to our assistance, at some point the rest of the world would realize they would be eliminated, it was inevitable. Mankind could not exist with different evolved human models for a long period of time particularly when one model was so much more intelligent and endowed with powers.

The Elders showed great interest in our attempts to stop the attacks with our lasers. A lot of the time was spent laughing about all the things we "zapped." They found it hysterical the way we described the military trying to figure out where their tanks had gone. They asked us several times to repeat the story and each time they laughed even louder.

Daniel asked how long it would take to get to our new planet? Shek, answered the planet was four light years away and it would take about twenty-five earth years. I asked why we were not being placed on Mars? EL said Mars was in the development path of mankind. There would eventually be a conflict. Mars could barely sustain life. Our new planet was very much like Earth.

I asked will we be able to join you in exploring the universe? Everyone laughed. Then Yashi said "Let's not rush things, first things first. Set up your planet, and then we'll see." This excited all of us very much. We could already see ourselves exploring. Yashi told Daniel he would have to be the Elder of our planet and we should have eight other Elders. He walked over to Daniel and put a six-pointed star medallion around his neck. Everyone applauded.

Daniel asked about our aging during the journey? Shek replied not to worry they had complete control over aging and death. Death was not a problem and aging would be minimal. I jokingly asked if they have any enemies in the universe? They all laughed. Yashi explained "enemies implied hatred and hatred destroys itself. Hatred could never attain the universe because the universe only reveals itself to love. Love which brings unlimited cooperation to achieve goals." Trying to hurt others destroys any individual and all such societies. A society built on hate can't progress because it is always destroying itself."

EL explained how there were four different planets that have achieved universal love. Their representatives were on "this ship and all ships exploring the universe." We had already noticed different physical races. They explained "there is only one mind in the universe, but it is only accessible through love." EL said we are the fifth group in the universe to attain it. And they were so happy to have our company. They were pleased to see how diverse culturally our group was. Daniel said it was a shame humanity didn't understand it is one race with different cultures. The rest of the meeting was very pleasant, we felt at home and laughed a lot.

On the third day, we returned to Earth. Every one gathered to hear of our experiences. They were thrilled by our description of the ship. But most of all, the thought of some day exploring the universe was most thrilling. Daniel looked at the group and said, "Scotty, beam me up." Everyone just laughed.

Email to Washington:
_____

Daniel and the other leaders have returned to Earth. They have been on the mother ship for three days. No doubt they were going over the plans to take over the planet. We can see Daniel organizing his followers and giving out assignments. He gave a speech to the entire town who stood like they were zombies. He is probably controlling their minds. After they take the planet, most of them will be eliminated, I'm sure. We can see from the faces of his family how enthusiastic they are to commence their attack. They seem to be packing. They have just this morning had all their farm equipment loaded onto the spaceship and taken up to the mother ship. They are also emptying their warehouses into container trucks and they also are being transported up to the mother ship, truck and all. They are transporting their vehicles up also. They probably don't want them damaged when the battle begins. My crew is standing by and are ready to stop them in any way we can. God help us.

We had many things to set up and a few committees to form:

First, we conveyed the request of the Elders that we choose our own Elders. Immediately everyone said Daniel should be our main Elder. They then went into discussion an hour later presenting their unanimous choices. I was so honored because they picked me, Mitchell, Vinny, Tom, Gary, Stan, Paige, Ebana, Asha, and Sharon. They explained to us how for so many years they had watched us work so hard for the betterment of the group. They all felt we were the most logical choices because of our direct connection to EL. We were very honored and said we hoped we would live up to their trust.

Our next task was to form a calendar committee our new world will have 480 days. That is how long it takes our new planet to go around its sun. The first day we arrive will start our calendar, our New Year's Day. The committee would have to figure out the names for the sixteen months. Also, for the days of the week. But Daniel insisted every month have two holidays. He also insisted we include Thanksgiving, Halloween, Xmas, Chanukah, New Years, the Fourth of July, and a day called EL day. Asha said how about Diwali? Daniel laughed and said why not? The committee had twenty-five years to finish. Daniel insisted we needed a whole week in each year to celebrate our passage from Earth to our new planet. We should tell our children of our struggles and accomplishments on Earth. We should speak of EL and how he came to our rescue, in that way we will always remember who we are and where we came from.

We needed a committee to organize our activities on the spaceship.
We needed a committee to run our schools.
We needed a committee to organize our sports

In this way we were preparing for the journey and our arrival to our new home. One other thing our new planet needed was a name so we created a naming committee.

When boarding the ship everyone was allowed to bring anything they wanted. We brought copies of the entire Library of Congress. We brought copies of all the movies we could get. Daniel asked our financial department to transfer royalties to the studios. We also brought dogs, cats, birds, sheep, chickens, horses, and other domesticated animals. Daniel made sure we had a supply of every plant seed in the world.

Whatever we thought we would need we brought. What we didn't have we acquired. We drove convoys out to warehouses and took what we needed. We emptied many warehouses of food, electrical equipment, we made sure we had thousands of our own fuel cells. It was a good thing we had made so many of them. We emptied warehouses full of pampers, baby food, beds and bedding. It must have been a strange sight to the crowds of onlookers watching us go out and take whatever we wanted. We paid for everything by wire transfer. The government could do nothing to stop us. We waved to everyone warmly. They stood there watching while everything was loaded in our trucks and we returned to our town.

Email to Washington:

They are leaving the perimeter of their town and stealing large quantities of supplies. I have ordered our forces to begin burning all warehouses in California to deprive them of anything they might need. We are also burning crops to deny them access to food they might want to take. If they want a fight, I'll give it to them. Maybe you should get the President to order a scorched earth policy across the nation. We must destroy anything we think they might use against us. By the way, they are Jews. We have a photo of Daniel and he is openly wearing a Star of David. My men have begun killing male Jews here in California. You should urge the President to do the same across the country. Once the attacks begin, I'm sure all the Jews will show their true colors and attack us. We knew it all along.

We down loaded all the data in the world we could find. Everything we could think of, we took. We where almost ready to leave when Carol got word Sailor was coming. We sent out a patrol to get him. His family did not come. They had other children and this was their home. When he arrived, he jokingly said he knew he and Carol will have a wonderful life together so long as she doesn't "scream" at him. We all laughed.

There was the question of what to do with our wealth, the gold, the money, and the real estate? We had our finance committee distribute our money and companies to trustworthy groups so their projects could continue. I made sure that Sailor's family was taken care of. Sailor's father was the CEO of an accounting company; his firm was given a large but little known charity that paid tuition for bright students. We transferred funds to all our charities. All the people whose mortgage were held by any of our companies received a letter of satisfaction so they held the property free and clear.

We intended to leave the town intact with the schools, the hospital, laboratories and the generating plant running. Our attorneys drew up papers deeding everything to the University of California. Secretly the papers were electronically recorded in the state records. Also, a copy was sent to the university.

We notified the Governor of California and the President of California State University to be on the perimeter of our town on September 3, Labor Day. The governor should bring a large force of state police with him. On that date we will lift the barrier and they will be able to enter the town. We explained that the town and everything that is in it, including the portfolio of the town, belong to the University of California. The troops were needed to prevent looting.

Email to Washington:

The idiot Governor of California has notified his state police that they are entering the alien town on Labor Day. Do you believe that arrogant liberal son of a bitch? Just because they paid for him to be elected, he thinks they are just going to open the door and let him in. He is telling everyone that they are leaving the entire town to the University of California and the police will secure it and protect it during the transfer. Boy, does he have an imagination. We are here defending America and he thinks they are just leaving and leaving it all to him.

Remember we could make gold; well, we had about a trillion dollars in gold and other metals located around the world. We arranged to have the ownership certificates dropped off at the various universities nearest the gold. (Harvard, MIT, Boston U, Cambridge, Oxford, Berlin, The Sorbonne, and others, they received about fifty billion each.) In total there were a few hundred universities that shared the pot. The gold was transferred to the universities by certificate of deposit which appeared in the depository records with each school's name attached. We deeded our estates and homes near the universities to the schools. The deeds were recorded in the county records and the school received a copy. Actually, it appeared as if the schools owned the property all along. The three buildings in Manhattan one was left to Ebana's family—"they couldn't leave New York." Of the other two, one went to NYU and the other to Columbia University.

Email to Washington:

We can see them loading up the smaller ships and delivering all the supplies they have stolen to the mother ship. Curiously, they have begun to board the mother ship. Almost the whole town has gone up. They are probably going to attack using the main ship, in that way they can guarantee they won't hit their own kind. After they wipe us out, they will take all the resources from the earth. That is probably what they were after all along. They are probably going to enslave our population to do the mining for them. Remember that movie where the people are controlled with drugs and forced to live underground mining for the aliens. In the end the people were able to fight back and eventually defeated the aliens. That is why I have hidden an enormous number of weapons all over the Rocky Mountains. It cost a lot, but we are ready. I'll keep you posted.

The day finally came when we were to board the spaceship, jokingly we called it "Daniel's Ark." Most of the people were already on board. We planned to be the last to leave. There were about two hundred of us. Daniel's whole family, Mitchell's, Sharon's all the original group from the hospital and my whole family. We would be the last to board. At the last minute, Daniel said "Let's go to the beach." We stared at him, then said why not? Getting into our cars we drove the twenty miles. It was a beautiful day to take a swim. Not a cloud in the sky. We were there about two hours, when Daniel said, "I guess we must go."

We were cleaning up and starting to get in the cars when we realized Daniel and his family were walking off the beach onto the highway. We all ran to catch up. The mob of people staring at us just parted on both sides of the highway. Everyone was very quiet. There were a lot of soldiers and we noticed as Daniel approached, they put down their weapons. In fact, they were placing them on the ground.

One of Daniel's grandsons asked, "Where we going, Grandpa?"

Daniel looked at him smiled and said "We are going home." I could see Daniel was crying.

At one point someone started singing "America the Beautiful." I could hear Daniel, with tears in his voice, almost screaming the words "Oh beautiful for…." It was a long walk for some of the kids, but they understood. We were going home. The thousands of people we had passed had formed in behind us and were marching and singing with us. Song after song, "God Bless America," "The Star Spangle Banner," "My Country This of Thee," "Over There," and others. They understood we were leaving, and they appeared to be sad.

On the journey a young man in a wheelchair rolled over to Daniel crying. He said "They don't understand, forgive them. Most of us love you, we realize you have to leave, but I'm grateful you were at least here. Thank you." Daniel stopped and bent over and held the fellow in his arms, they both were crying as the young man stood up and slowly joined us on our journey. He walked next to Daniel holding his hand. At our border Daniel asked him if he wanted to come? He hugged Daniel and said, "I must stay. I have family and more importantly, I don't want anyone to forget you were here." They hugged again and we walked through our barrier and boarded our ship.

Email to Washington:

I can't believe our military. Daniel and his entire family went to the beach, they stayed about an hour and decided to walk

back to their town. It was a parade. The thousands of spec-
tators and all the military personnel simply stepped aside as
they passed. What is worse is that the soldiers put down their
weapons. I mean literally they laid their weapons on the
ground. It was absurd. Daniel at the head of this mob singing
"God Bless America" and all those thousands of people in-
cluding our military marching behind them singing "Amer-
ica the Beautiful" and other bullshit songs. It was sickening.
He must have used mass hypnosis on the crowd. There is
something else we have to worry about when the attack be-
gins, "mass hypnosis." He might just take control of the minds
of our forces and enslave them. I'll keep you posted.

Our shields remained around our town until we were a safe distance from Earth. On September 3, Labor Day, a signal was sent that literally disintegrated every trace of our technology that could be used as a weapon. Everything completely turned to dust. There was no way the government could get hold of any of it.

From on board the ship, we monitored the earth as we were traveling through space. Shortly after we departed, the governments of various countries began to round up all the intellectuals and put them in prison. In some cases, they were killed. They also rounded up many young people. Universities were closed. Some humanitarian projects were shut down. A lot of the workers were killed. The internet was shut down but only for a sort time. The government said they shutdown the internet because scientists thought we could physically harm humans by transmissions from outer space.

Email to Washington:
They're gone. They just packed up their bags, got on their
space ship and left. We won! It was a long battle, but in the
end, they realized we would not leave them in peace. They
would always have to face our opposition. It's a great relief.

A great victory. We really did it. I'm sure the President will recognize that we are the reason for this great victory. We may even get a medal. Actually, I'm ready to retire, collect my pension and maybe write a book about the long battle we waged against those aliens. My only regret is that I never got my hands on Kate. I'm sure it would have been a great pleasure. I am going to wind up our operation on the West Coast. What do I do with all the money we have?

(With all the damage this idiot caused he regrets that he didn't get hold of me?)

Even though we left on our own, the government was taking credit for defeating us. They demonstrated this by rounding up and killing anyone who seemed to support us. Unfortunately, the Jewish communities around the globe were attacked. There were demonstration and mobs beating up anyone who seemed smart. There were people happy to see those "alien sympathizers taken care of." The newspapers headlines read, "aliens on the run."

The government claimed they had "run off the aliens." They boasted of how the military should be honored for the great service and sacrifice it made. How they had held off and defeated the aliens. They praised all the service personnel killed defending democracy. A special medal was struck and issued to the "hero" service personnel who had held off the "alien offensive." It was called the EARTH DEFENSE MEDAL.

We were sad because there was nothing we could do to help. We were on our way to a new life. We could only hope evolution would take care of the continued development of new-world consciousness. Daniel said the change could not be totally eliminated so long as the women survive. It will be passed on. It would reappear and eventually humanity would join us in the universe. We hoped it would not be too far in the future.

Safe aboard the ship we have begun our new lives. This record of our experiences on Earth is meant to help the future and inspire young people to follow the truth through the path of love, a path that opens the universe.

Email from Washington:

You have to come to Washington. The President is listening to the Director of the CIA. I found out that he went to Harvard with Daniel and his group. That is why he is so sympathetic to them. The President wants a full report. He wants to know where was the alien attack? How is it that we committed so much of our resources to a cause that never materialized? They want a full accounting of all our assets and a complete budget report. Somehow the President found out about the billions we got when we seized the alien assets. They even know about our mountain retreat. I'm sure it's the CIA that has supplied the President with that info. They want to know why you burned down half of California. I never gave you authorization to do that. There is also a matter of you ordering the murder of Jewish families in California. They have a copy of your memo to your agents. I certainly did not authorize that. In short, we are in trouble.

Email from Washington continued:

We knew all along we would not be recognized for the great effort we expended defending America. These sons of bitches in Washington are just looking for scapegoats to take the blame for the loss of a few warehouses. They really don't understand. The only reason those aliens did not take over the earth was our persistent attacks that kept them on the defensive. Realize, they are probably going to retire us without even giving us a watch. Try to be here tomorrow, I think we should look into the possibility that we might need attorneys. They are on a witch hunt and we are easy targets now that we have eliminated the aliens as a threat. For my part I will not go down without a fight. These bastards just don't understand that we saved humanity. Get here quickly so we can plot strategy.

MEMO: TOP SECRET

REFERENCE OUR LAST CONVERSATION: WE DO NOT WANT THOSE TWO IDIOTS COMING TOGETHER IN WASHINGTON TO EMBARRASS THE PRESIDENT WITH THEIR STUPID THEORY THAT THEY DROVE OUT THE ALIENS WE CERTAINLY DON'T WANT THEM CLAIMING THEY WERE AUTHORIZED TO CARRY OUT THE ATROC-ITIES THEY DID.

THEY ARE TO BE ELIMINATED. MAKE IT LOOK NATU-RAL. ONCE THEY ARE GONE, WE WILL POINT OUT THEY WERE A ROUGE OPERATION USING STOLEN MONEY TO FURTHER THEIR OWN AMBITIONS.

DELETE AFTER READING

Dear Mr. Stanley Stainer,

Daniel suggested I send you this story. We loved the way you treated EL and us in your movie. If you are reading this it is because we encoded the transmission to pick up your DNA before it would download. We hope you can use this material without getting in any trouble. If you do make a movie, I'm sure we would love it. Anyway, this is Kathy and Daniel and our entire group saying goodbye and thank you.

P.S. We have transferred five hundred million dollars to your company as a way of thanking you for the wonderful movie and to encourage you to tell the world our story.

Thank you again,
Kathy, Daniel's sister.